A LIKELY STORY

ERIC WRIGHT

A LIKELY STORY

A JOE BARLEY MYSTERY

Cormorant Books

This is a first edition.

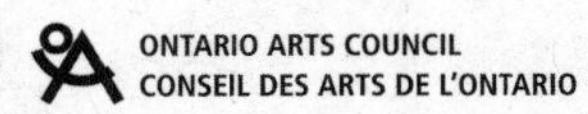

The publisher gratefully acknowledges the support of the Canada Council for the Arts and the Ontario Arts Council for its publishing program. We acknowledge the financial support of the Government of Canada through the Canada Book Fund for our publishing activities.

Printed and bound in Canada

LIBRARY AND ARCHIVES CANADA CATALOGUING IN PUBLICATION

Wright, Eric

A likely story : a Joe Barley mystery / Eric Wright.

ISBN 978-1-897151-86-0

I. Title.

PS8595.R58L54 2010 C813'.54 C2010-903990-4

Cover art and design: Angel Guerra/Archetype
Interior text design: Tannice Goddard, Soul Oasis Networking
Printer: Transcontinental

The text pages of this book are printed on 100% post-consumer waste recycled paper.

CORMORANT BOOKS INC.
215 SPADINA AVENUE, STUDIO 230, TORONTO, ON CANADA M5T 2C7
www.cormorantbooks.com

For Richard

CHAPTER ONE

THE NIGHT THEY TOOK THE first car, I was driving to work as usual to be at my office by six, which meant driving across town during rush hour, always an ordeal because I've never felt at home behind the wheel. On this night, though, I was on automatic pilot. I left my apartment and arrived at the college parking lot with no memory of having negotiated any part of the trip — making all the turns, changing lanes, stopping at the red lights — all because I was trying to think about Carole, my partner, now well into the last weeks of her pregnancy and us not yet started looking for a cradle, or me for a regular job.

My name is Joe Barley. I'm a part-time instructor in the English department at Hambleton, a college in the east end of Toronto where I have been for too many years, hoping for a proper appointment with pension rights and sabbaticals and a course of my own. I have finally accepted that it isn't going to happen, that this is probably my last year at Hambleton, even as a part-timer, unless an epidemic wipes out my colleagues.

This morning, the subject of Carole's pregnancy having been introduced subliminally by my noticing the trouble she was having squeezing through the space between the refrigerator and the kitchen table, I said, "Anything happening yet?"

"Like what?"

I said, "Let's have an agreement that if you don't know what I'm talking about then you know what I'm talking about." I pointed at her navel. "In there."

She leaned back against the kitchen counter, smiled, patted her belly, and said, "Nothing I could identify."

The message I got from this was that she was still happy with her situation, just watchful, certainly not worried; content.

We were an item, Carole and me, unmarried but certainly hitched. According to her sister and brother-in-law, both psychiatrists, we were bound together by our insecurities, mostly mine. Life without her would be unthinkable, and I know that she feels the same. Given the number of ways a marriage or its equivalent can screw up these days as the generation quests in search of perfect sex — how goes your orgasm lately? — I had recently been counting myself extraordinarily lucky — and it *is* luck — in arriving at the right time with the right person able to say, this is it, it won't get any better. I was right: we'd done it by instinct and indulged in very little in the way of self-analysis. The fact is, we'd blundered into the good life. Though neither one of us had actually lived with anyone else before we met, both of us had backed out of one or two blind alleys, and after a very nervous beginning our present situation had become secure over the last five years.

We knew, though, that at some point we had to make our luck permanent. We had come together without romance, in curiosity, really, and for a long time I didn't know if she was for keeps until we had a misunderstanding that shook her into revealing what she felt about me, showing herself to me naked, as it were, and in tears. We have never referred to that day again, so the opportunity to create a fuller dialogue of understanding was let go.

And so, although we were certain of each other's hearts, the minds still waited to be explored. For example, I was surprised in the recent election to find that she is both apolitical and much further to the left than anyone we know, but she is no longer engaged in the process. She almost forgot to vote, and when she did go into the booth it was to put a cross for the Green candidate. She isn't active in support of the Greens between elections because she sees the ecological situation as hopeless so long as there is money to be made out of poisoning the earth, the air, and the water. She does nothing to make things worse, like buying newspapers, but doesn't waste her time trying to make things better. For her, the future will be determined by nuclear mistakes and manufactured plagues and there is nothing to be done about it. The daily pleasures — books, prepared foods from Pusateri and the Summerhill Market, and me — are enough to be thankful for. Let Armageddon take care of itself.

Then she got pregnant.

When she first made the announcement, I said "How did it happen?"

She grabbed the chance. "Well," she said, in the bright voice of a cartoon chipmunk, "First of all, as my old granny advised me, I had a nice all-over wash, then ironed my favourite nightie and sprinkled it with lavender water. Then you took off your pants and put out the light ..."

"All right, all right. You really think it's happened?"

"You think I'm rehearsing for a play? Yes, I have the symptoms of pregnancy."

"Are you surprised?"

"No."

"You've been expecting this?"

"I thought it might happen."

"And now it has happened. Are you terrified, alarmed, worried, curious, pleased, or ecstatic?"

"It sounds as if you've been rehearsing. All of the above."

"When will you prefer one of these emotions?"

"I'm waiting to find out."

"Is there a good chance you'll be 'pleased'?"

"Yes."

"So there's no chance you will want to have an —"

"I've already passed that point, in my head."

"This is not an intellectual pro-life decision you've found?"

"I am all in favour of people not having unwanted babies, even if it's just because they don't want them."

"So we are going to have a baby."

"Unless I miscarry. Very common with old women like me."

Carole is thirty-eight.

"If that happens, we're back to square one?"

"That's right. Maybe square two. I'll have had a major experience and no consequences to cope with."

"But assuming you go the distance, what then?"

"I'll have a baby. A little bastard."

"We'll have a baby."

"Right. I didn't hear it first time." She stroked her belly. "That 'we' is good news."

"Of course it's 'we.'"

"I wasn't sure. It was never in our plans."

"We never had any plans. We'll have to make some."

"Like grown-ups, you mean? Soon I'll be able to look at those girls with baby-carriages, eighteen and nineteen some of them, and tell myself I know as much about life as they do."

"That's what I've been telling myself lately. 'Grow up,' I've been saying to myself. Now, how are we going to live?"

"What do you mean?"

"I'll need a permanent job."

"What about your novel?"

"I'll ask around, find out how married men with jobs get their novels written. Actually, this may be the excuse I've been looking for to abandon it. I'm sick of the characters, anyway."

"Do you think they'll fire you soon?"

"It's a question of whether they'll rehire me."

"Have you been thinking what you might do?'

"I'll start looking around tomorrow."

"Advertising? Journalism?"

"No and no. I'm too old to start in advertising. To the hotshots in that world, I would look grizzled. And I wouldn't know where to begin in journalism."

"You know what a counsellor would say? Treat this as an opportunity. I can support us both for a while. Think of something you'd like to do. Oh, sweetie." She produced a huge sob, smiled, and came over and put her arms around me and I thought, this is the first time she has ever called me that. She said, "I'm so happy. Find a way to join me." She kissed me then, and reached out and groped me conjugally, looking for a response to the new earthiness she was feeling.

CHAPTER TWO

I WOKE UP FROM MY reverie to see Tommy Stokoe, the campus security officer, crouched by the gate of the parking lot, holding up his hand. He peered through the windscreen then walked around to the side window. He said, "Park your car would you, Joe, and give me a minute."

I drove around the lot until I could find the kind of space I need if I'm going to manage to park the first time, and walked back to the gate where a small group of people now surrounded the security officer.

When I started at Hambleton I looked about for some other work to eke out my part-timer's salary and I found it with the Atkinson Detective Agency; low-level work, looking for husbands who haven't kept up their support payments mainly, the equivalent in status to my teaching position. Everyone in the college knows what I do when I'm not teaching, and it is this work that has brought Tommy Stokoe, our security boss, closer to me, though not me to him. For Stokoe I am the one person who might understand how hard his job is.

Now he said, "Need some information, Joe," and asked me questions to find out if I used the lot regularly, and if I had used it earlier that evening, and if I had at any time noticed anyone unusual in the area. An assistant, a uniformed security guard, stood ready to write down what I said. By the time Stokoe had finished questioning me, I gathered that a car had been stolen from the lot earlier by someone unknown.

As usual, he looked away from me as he spoke quietly out of the corner of his mouth, creating an air of talking in confidence. He even used this stance to pass on his opinion of the weather, and I had learned to look past it to listen to the words. And as usual he spoke rapidly and without punctuation to give as much of the backstory as he could before anyone could interrupt. "I mean Christ you'd think a guy would know when he arrived I mean shit most people leave home at the same time every day and take about the same time to get to work so when you ask them about it they can tell you when they usually get home at night at least maybe the time it usually takes and if there was anything different that held them up that day an accident maybe but not this clown he doesn't know what day it is." He licked a small fleck of spittle from the corner of his mouth and I got a word in edgewise.

"Who is it?"

"Professor Munchkin over there." He flicked his head in the direction of a man who was having his story taken down by a security guard: Vladimir Petrov, a professor of sociology, originally from Bulgaria, an extremely excitable man who was usually, and now obviously, beside himself. Petrov is a Marxist who allies himself with every student protest. I like him because he likes me because he thinks I'm a closet socialist who is denying his true nature.

"Joseph," he called (the only person, now my grandmother has died, who gives me both syllables), waving me towards him and swinging his shoulders around in an arc to claim a wider audience. "Joseph, will you please explain to these ...," he pointed to the security guards contemptuously before he remembered that all men, especially working-class men, are created equal, and forced a smile, "... people that forgetting where you parked your car is not an offence against the state?"

"You can't remember where you parked?"

"Better than that, Joseph. I can't remember *when* I parked." He looked triumphant.

The two guards waited silently. Vladimir turned and took a couple of steps away from us to give himself more room to wave his arms about, and flicked a finger at the guards in a "You-may-now-speak" gesture. Vladimir was born into the Bulgarian aristocracy, or, at least, into their landed gentry, and in times of stress his heritage overcomes his acquired political convictions. Still he had probably built up some credit with the guards in previous encounters — he likes getting down and dirty with them to show his egalitarianism; they in turn seem to regard him with affection. They have nicknamed him The Count.

Now one of the guards, who was trying to take notes, spoke. "We're not sure when the car was stolen because Professor Petrov can't tell us when he last saw it. Seems he might have left it here overnight." He consulted his notes as the other guard looked at the sky. "Says he came out of class this afternoon, and when he went to drive home, he couldn't find his car. This was about three-thirty, sir?"

Vladimir nodded from a distance.

The guard continued. "Not being able to find it in his usual spot, he assumed he hadn't brought it today."

The other guard seemed to be choking.

"But when he got home the car wasn't in the parking space in front of his house, either. Then he remembered coming to the college on the subway this morning — subway and bus, that is. He distinctly remembers the bus, don't you sir?" he added, smiling.

"So the car disappeared from his house?"

"Well, no, sir, see, he also distinctly remembers coming to work by car yesterday because he gave a ride to a neighbour."

"But he didn't drive home yesterday?" I was going to be late for work.

"Seems not, no."

I turned to Petrov, who had paused to listen to this discussion of his movements. "So, Vladimir, the car disappeared sometime between yesterday morning, when you arrived at the college, and this afternoon, when you tried to go home. Probably stolen."

"Unless Professor Petrov left it somewhere else." Both guards were grinning steadily now, having fun.

"Vladimir?"

"I am a creature of habit. If I had changed my routine I would haf remembered, and also why. I went home on the subway yesterday, forgetting I had my car here. I came to the college by subway today, intending to drive home. But when I came to the parking lot this afternoon I could not find my car, so you see I then thought perhaps I did drive home yesterday and had parked it on my street. I was very tired, and the entrance to the parking space at my house is very narrow and obscured by a utility pole which has been known to leap out and scrape the side of my car, especially when I am tired. But this morning the citizen in me took over from the professor, and, not seeing the car on the street, I assumed I had left it here in order to safely haf a couple of beers after work. Which I only do when I don't bring the car." He smiled sweetly at us, all the little near-jokes showing he was enjoying himself now.

Vladimir's English teacher in Sofia had been an Oxford man, a public school man, too, I would think, because Vladimir speaks whole sentences like a true Wykehamist — grammar, landed-gentry accent, the lot — but then, somewhere in the middle of a paragraph, the Bulgarian sidles in with a "haf" instead of a "have." But his Bulgarian accent is most marked when he is unstressed, which makes me suspect that it is entirely under his control, that he is doing it for fun.

The guard with the notebook said, "Here's the cavalry now. I'll report all this to the boss." He gestured to the gate of the parking lot, where Tommy Stokoe was talking to a city cop in a squad car. The guard said, "If it's lost, they'll find it, if it's stolen ..."

"They won't," his colleague said, still grinning.

None of this was remarkable. As Tommy said, "We've all done it shit forgotten that we brought the car or left it at home well not me of course but it happens point is the car was here all night probably when the lot was empty so it would be a great temptation for a lot of jerk-offs and there are plenty of those hereabouts shit our security was never designed for a thing like this we don't have enough people on the ground see ..."

But as he began the next tape, about how he manages his limited resources, I constructed a way to share an immediate concern with Petrov who was now on his way out of the parking lot.

"Vladimir," I called, pressing Tommy's arm to show how much I would like to have stayed if I hadn't had to share something of life-or-death importance with the sociologist. "Wait for me!"

He stopped and stared at me. "Someone has stolen my car!" he said.

"Yes, I know. I was there. You don't think ...?" I was going to suggest that he might have loaned it to someone, or left it in a garage for servicing. Or simply left it in a parking lot on the other side of town. All these were possible and not just with Petrov. The best campus story on this topic is of the professor of geography who drove down to the municipal offices to protest a parking ticket, had his protest accepted and the parking ticket cancelled, then went home in triumph on the subway, leaving his car all night on King Street, where the parking police found it, towed it away, and charged him two hundred and twenty dollars to get it back.

But the suggestion sounded rude as I formed it up, because I did actually think Vladimir was a bit of a nutcase.

He saved me by shaking his head seven or eight times. "No, no, no, no. I remember clearly now. I came with my car yesterday and parked next to that woman in Nursing. Carmela."

"Black is beautiful?" I said, automatically.

"What?"

I regretted the words immediately. They phrased a compliment that a few of us in the English department paid to a shimmering beauty from Trinidad who taught in the Health Sciences department, a nurse. They were first uttered by a Philosophy instructor, who further offered that she made him feel like the hunchback of Notre Dame, or someone from an inferior, much uglier species who belonged in a cage. Bert Crabtree, the philosopher, was just exaggerating to make a point but these days anything said by man of woman goes into the language laboratory to be sifted for trace elements of racism or sexism. Crabtree's description of the Trinidad beauty is still preserved among a few close friends, but it wasn't to be trusted to Petrov.

I said, "I'm sorry, Vladimir. I was thinking of something else, an ad I saw for a new car. You might have to get one. A new car. You've got complete coverage?"

"Of course not. I buy old cars and insure them only for third parties. Insurance is a racket, run by the richest companies in the world. Let me tell you something, Joseph; my neighbour had his car stolen, and when he reported it to the insurance company they told him he was entitled to a rental car — he had paid an extra premium for this — but if his own car was recovered undamaged he would have to pay back the cost of the rental. The company assumes, of course, that my neighbour is a crook, like them, and would pretend to have lost the car in order to have another one for a while, an extra one, for his wife, perhaps."

"Will you look for another Ford?" I asked, to cut him off. Most of the faculty in the Humanities' departments drive European or Japanese cars on the orders of consumer magazines, but Petrov, I knew, supported Canadian factory workers and their products.

"Probably. Is there a subtext to that question?"

Flags were everywhere waiting to go up. I said, "Not that I'm aware of, but there's no such thing as an innocent question, is there? I'll try another thought, equally without a subtext. Are you teaching tonight?"

"I just came back to see if I had left my car here after all. Now I am going to my office so that I can start going home again." He smiled widely to show that now he was really making fun of himself.

"Perhaps," I said, "as you are preparink to leaf, your body's memory will direct you down a different path to the place where you parked your car." I was appalled to hear myself speaking with a touch of a mock-Bulgarian accent, already polishing the story to relate it to Carole.

But Vladimir didn't hear it. "Perhaps," he said. "That is what I meant."

IN MY OFFICE, I LOOKED around for something to do. A few potential students had sent queries about the courses to be offered next year, and one former student had asked for a copy of his record to apply for accreditation at some other institute. There was a request from the instructor teaching business correspondence to see me after class. And that was it. About fifteen minutes before I could get on with my novel.

It hadn't gone well for some time, not as a novel, that is. The writing was in its second year and had reached a crucial stage — the middle, I hoped. I was bored to numbness with it, but every time I thought of abandoning it I read it through early in the day and found some serviceable bits of writing here and there and pressed on again, hoping to find more. After all, *Madam Bovary* took ten years, didn't it?

I am hired by the session to teach whatever is left over after the chairman has made up the timetables of the tenured faculty. This year I've been given two courses in the day program, but two courses at the hourly rate aren't enough to live on so the chairman found me three hours teaching remedial English to foreign students, and then added a tiny (paid) administrative responsibility, appointing me coordinator of non-credit English courses in the extension program, a sinecure with almost no work attached. (He's a nice guy, my chairman, but in giving me this little job he has reached the limits of his power to help me.) Subsequently, too few students registered for my night course and it was cancelled, but the position of coordinator remained in the budget. I don't usually have to stay the whole evening.

To sum it up, my position is bleak. I am looking for a regular full-time permanent job without any qualifications except those in plentiful supply and with no real experience of any kind of work other than teaching English. I am like a middle-aged nun whose vocation has been taken away from her and now is to be led to the gates of the convent to fend for herself. It's my fault; I know; I just went on hoping for too long.

I put the manuscript of the novel aside after twenty minutes and started to prepare my day courses. At nine o'clock, the man with the appointment, David Simmonds, my teacher of Business Correspondence, arrived.

Simmonds had been hired as we experienced a sudden unexpected surge in enrolment in the "correspondence for business" course. Most of the extension classes are assigned to instructors in the spring; then, in the fall, close to the beginning of the term, we look at the enrolment to see how many extra sections we might need. Thus it was that Simmonds appeared so fortuitously in answer to a need for an additional instructor at the beginning of term. He had been recommended by someone in the administration, and had given me no problems so far, itself a great recommendation for a new instructor in the extension program.

I remembered that he had not shined himself up much for the hiring interview; alternatively, he may have dressed very carefully. He was very tall, perhaps six feet three or four, dressed in khakis and a leather blazer over a blue denim shirt, all of his clothes very new. He was bald across the top of his head, with thick black hair sprouting at either side, a heavy, ragged moustache, and elsewhere, dark stubble. Seen through eyes older than mine he might have looked like someone on the fringes of society who had been given fresh clothes by a welfare agency in order to get this job, but to his own generation he could just as easily have been a television presenter, as long as he remained seated.

Because almost immediately, just in sitting down, he showed an extraordinary clumsiness. He had these very large feet laced up in strong brown boots that seemed to have a mind of their own. As he sat down, one of his boots went sideways to kick over a wastebasket that was only just in his way, making him look down in surprise at what was going on down there, and when he left, the boots seemed to clear their own path to the door, taking their instructions from his knees, while his hands locked up his briefcase and then tried to straighten out his coat collar, which had twisted itself under his coat.

I asked him about his experience. He said he was an office manager, had written a lot of letters.

"But teaching?" I asked.

He said he had to show the new clerks how to write a letter.

"But no actual lectern experience?"

"Is it so hard?" he responded, not aggressively, but not really wanting to know, either. Rhetorically. Then he added, "College teaching isn't like high school, is it? You don't have to be trained for it. You learn whatever tricks you need on the job, right?"

"More or less," I said.

He waited for me then. He'd made his point. We all have to start somewhere, and teaching correspondence for business at night was surely close to the bottom rung.

I thought, all right, the one thing certain was that he felt sure of himself, which is nine-tenths of the game in teaching; the rest is knowing something.

He sat still, smiling mechanically at my jokes, but not making any of his own, showing his comfort, not so much by his body language as by the absence of any body language. But his record was adequate, he spoke more or less grammatically, and his own letter of application for the job was flawless. I remember asking him if Toronto was his hometown, and he said, no, he came from Edmonton.

Now I waited while he explained his problem. He had two students registered in his class he wanted to get rid of. I said, "I don't think we can actually get rid of anyone in a non-credit extension course unless they are disturbing the other students. Mostly they just go away."

"These clowns are unteachable. They've skipped half the classes, and they're taking up space. They'll have to go." He leaned back in his chair and looked around the room while I considered the problem. He wasn't asking for my decision, just explaining what I had to do.

"Who are they?"

He opened his briefcase to take out a sheet of paper, then dropped the briefcase, spilling its contents over the floor.

I came around the desk to help him pick up, hoping not to find any half-eaten sandwiches on the floor, or miniature bottles of vodka, or ointment for hemorrhoids. There was nothing except the paperwork of a class.

He took his time about sorting the paper into a sequence before returning it to his briefcase, leaving himself with a single sheet. "Clem Downie and Jack Zimmerman," he read. He handed over the piece of paper with the names printed on.

"They sound familiar."

"They're a pair. They came together. They play hockey, remember?"

Of course. The hockey players, brought to the school by the head of Physical Education at the urging of the president, awarded the nearest thing Hambleton has to an athletic scholarship, dreamed up by the president himself. The president dearly wanted us to win a cup or a league or something. Just one game would do, for starters.

I said, "It was the president's idea, to give athletes too poor to pay the fees a chance to get into the education stream. Like late bloomers."

"I know the story, and I know the real reason, but why me? Why did they get put into my class? It's a good group, all mature students." Now Simmonds belched, louder than I've heard anyone belch in an office before. He looked around the room as he waited for my answer.

I smiled with automatic tolerance. I said, "These boys needed something easy and structured. I've taught your course. I thought you could adapt the principles to any level."

"Not to these guys. The Slapshot Boys. You know?"

"I saw the movie. I'm sorry. Maybe they'll go away."

"They keep going away, but they always come back. They were there tonight, after the break."

"The game with Sudbury Teacher's College is coming up and they have to attend a certain number of classes to qualify as students. It's an ordinary league game, actually, but a big one for us — the first that we might have a chance of winning, I hear."

"Can't we give them their money back?" Now Simmonds began to hear that the solution to his problem might be harder than he had thought. This was the world of higher education — of a kind — not whatever world he was used to.

"They're here on scholarships. *We're* paying *them*."

"Jesus." Simmonds stood up, knocking over his chair behind him. "I'm wasting my time even talking about it, I guess. I'll give them a packet of crayons and put them in the corner." He set the chair on its legs.

There was nothing I could do for him. The awarding of hockey scholarships was just one of the ideas the new president has dreamed up to boost the public's awareness and possibly the status of the college. Among other proposals that had come out of his office were suggestions for several new disciplines — even "Graduate Studies" was being whispered. A winning, or at least a competitive, hockey team that would be noticed by the *Toronto Star* fitted the president's dream of the future. All he wanted was to be allowed to sit at the same table as the big boys. He would not mind being least among equals, at first.

"Are they creating a disturbance?"

"Yeah, just by being there. And the language. They treat the place like a changing room. Hey, that's neat." He was standing in front of the only picture I have hung in my office, one that Carole had given me as a joke. It was a greeting card that she had had framed to cheer up the room, the well-known picture of a pig taking off from a springboard over a pond.

I tried again. "Are they a real problem? Can you handle them?"

He turned to look at me, still thinking about the pig. "Huh? Oh, I can *handle* them. I grew up with guys like them. They're just a pain in the ass." He nodded. "Take it easy," he said, and was gone.

And that was the last I saw of him for two weeks. He disappeared, leaving a note but no forwarding address.

When he reappeared he was wearing granny glasses and a gold earring, sitting in his car outside the building.

"Professor?" A man with a ladder stood in the doorway, holding a light bulb, ready to replace one that had burned out. I stuffed the manuscript into my briefcase and left.

CHAPTER THREE

WHEN I GOT HOME, CAROLE was in bed, reading, and eating a granola bar. This was normal. Carole spends most of her free time reading. We go to a lot of movies, but otherwise she reads.

She reads voraciously and actively, reading even obviously crappy books so that she can articulate why they are crappy. Sometimes she reads and rereads books she actively dislikes, like most of James Joyce's work, because she hasn't figured out what is wrong with it, but she will do that only if the book is universally praised, like *A Portrait of the Artist as a Young Man*, and she admires extravagantly some other story by the same author. In the case of Joyce, the evidence that Joyce could write is the story, "The Dead." Happily, she doesn't insist on sharing her reading experiences with me. The last book I had taken note of was Goethe's *Elective Affinities*, a novel she had once pronounced unreadable and was now reading for the third time.

"How's Goethe," I asked now, pronouncing the name "Go-Ethe" to keep my distance from it.

She showed me what she was reading now: *Full Moon*, a novel by P.G. Wodehouse.

"Ah-hah!" I said. "I distinctly remember you telling me, in the early days of our relationship, while we were still feeling each other out, that you were mystified by the esteem in which Wodehouse was held by many people you respected. Evelyn Waugh, for example. In those days you found Wodehouse silly, unfunny, and trivial. What's happened?"

"I think I've gone through a period of growth, like discovering how good Purcell is. Listen, here's a line from this book. 'From sheer force of habit, he started guiltily.' There, see?" she continued. "He puts two clichés together and produces a line worthy of that Irishman you like, the Atswimtwobirds man. Here's another, this time just a bit of description. One of the characters has received a telegram, warning him, 'Arriving tea time with landlady.' What would that be, he wonders, something stout in a sealskin coat and a Sunday bonnet? There: the whole thing in ten words."

I wondered what was going on. It sounded to me as if Carole's pregnancy was affecting her taste buds, but typically with Carole it was her literary tastes that had become distorted.

"So what's next?" I asked.

"I don't know." She put her book on the night table and pulled the duvet back around her chin, a gesture that meant "No more questions, please."

It was time for me to show I was still on her side. I climbed in beside her and curled myself around her and she snuggled back against me.

After a while, she said, "The doctor said there's still a way if you want."

I said, "I think I've got a headache," and she laughed.

I lay awake for an hour, mute and wondering, trying once more to think my way into the new world, a world with a partner, a child, and no steady job. As if to confirm that I had something to think about she stirred in her sleep and took my hand to stroke her belly.

For seven years she had been the solid and certain wage earner in our relationship, the one with a future and a pension plan. Our situation, that of the day-labouring husband and the professional wife (although we aren't actually married), is common in our world, especially where the husband is in his seventh year of graduate school or has artistic pretensions. I know of several. One of them, a couple we were closer to five or six years ago, started out in just this way. She qualified as a lawyer and started to make lawyer-type money. He went out cleaning offices, a job that left him free to think while he worked (he was trying to be a playwright). What happened then would be perfect material for a Somerset Maugham story, or even an O. Henry. In an amalgamation of law firms, she was first absorbed into the new firm and then fired, and found herself out of work for several months, being supported by her spouse, the office-cleaner. He, in the meantime, discovered a talent for office husbandry and soon was employing an army of workers, cleaning offices and washing windows, lately buying his first parking lot where he rents space for four dollars a half-hour. His wife now works as his office manager.

But I digress. To repeat, the situation of the professional wife propping up the "creative" (or scholar-apprentice) husband is common enough in my world, and I'd been happy in the role, but Carole's pregnancy and her reaction to it have forced me to try to think. We had never talked seriously about what we would do if our endeavours were blessed in the usual way, and so I had stayed with the assumption that Carole was making sure they never would be. It didn't cross my mind that she might deliberately have created the situation, or allowed it to happen, by which I mean that it crossed my mind very quickly, but I suppressed the thought because the implications of that were much more life-changing than a simple unplanned pregnancy.

CHAPTER FOUR

THE MORNING AFTER SHE TOLD me she was pregnant, eight months earlier, Carole woke up smiling, and at some other time I might have melted into her dream, but now it seemed unnatural, as if I would have been taking advantage of her apparently drugged condition — drugged by joy, it seemed.

I said, "Have you decided yet?"

"Decided what?" Carole said. "Tea or coffee? I'll make both."

I said, "How we're going to arrange the rest of our lives," then turned from her, dismissing the subject until she was in a different mood. "Can I have the bathroom first?"

"Are you teaching this morning? I thought this was a writing morning."

"I have to sort out a problem." I nearly added, "You."

"Meet you at six, then, at Loblaws." She started to hum.

She never hums; she doesn't know how; she can't even carry a tune. When the conversation turns to music, she borrows a joke from W.S. Gilbert, claiming she knows two tunes: one of them is "O Canada" and the other one isn't. Now she was humming like a cleaning woman from Gananoque we had once who used to hum as she polished, making a sound like an Inuit throat-singer warming up.

For the next eight months I watched in wonder as Carole's belly grew shiny and round like a cookbook illustration for a dome-shaped pudding. We were still charged with happy concupiscence. Having done no preparation for the event, I didn't know what to expect. I assumed that sooner or later, sooner probably, we would move into a celibate stage. What I got, and was still getting, was more joy than in a non-Christian heaven. I tried to be careful of the next generation (I was having trouble finding a term I could get comfortable with, something descriptive, human, and affectionate like "the young un" or "the nipper") and Carole promised, each time we embraced, that she would let me know when it was time to back off, but it hadn't happened yet. What *had* happened was that I was made aware of this other life growing between us, even as we made love, vividly so, when it/she/he started to move. It was literature, of course, that supplied the figure, the name, the idea, and then the reality of the "secret sharer." It spooked me for a while, until I became comfortable in the presence of the stranger within.

DURING THE YEARS THAT THE college hardened its attitude to part-timers without Ph.D.'s, the sessional appointees in the English department became distanced from the full-time faculty, rarely sharing in their joys and sorrows, or they in ours. It's a natural process: they had permanent jobs, and could think about literature, or rather, literary criticism; we didn't; we thought and talked mainly about finding work, itinerant labourers following the academic harvest. Now, the only part-timer left, I had become an outsider. On this day, feeling closer to Herb Mullins, our registrar, than to any of my tenured colleagues, I decided to drop in on him to seek some advice about the Slapshot Boys.

Tommy Stokoe and a security guard were again fussing around the gate of the parking lot as I drove up. Tommy held up his hand and I rolled down my window. He handed me a piece of paper, a notice, headed "Change of Parking Lot Card Keys." Before I could read it, he was telling me about it. "It's what you do after a theft-type infraction," he said, quietly, searching the horizon. "I mean I know it sounds like kind of locking-the-barn-door-after-they've-got-away type thing but we're all going hard as we can and I haven't got the manpower to watch the lot all night and this is only one of the four I'm responsible for anyway as I say it's standard procedure ..."

"Change the locks," I said, over the top of whatever he was saying next. "Good idea. Makes sense. Where do I get a new card?"

"It's all on that sheet I just gave you in your hand day after tomorrow they'll have them ready and you have to pick them up in person and identify yourself the trouble is ..."

Luckily, a cold November rain was coming down on him and I was blocking someone behind me so I drove to the first vacant spot and ran, looking at my watch, apparently late for my class and getting wet, past Tommy and his guard.

By the time I reached Herb Mullins's office I had worked out a reasonable excuse to waste his time.

As registrar, Herb is ultimately responsible for the students' marks, and a famous incident confirmed it. An instructor in Retail Merchandising had awarded grades to his students that were so far out of line with the grades the students had earned in other subjects as to suggest that the instructor was having a breakdown (which turned out to be what was happening), and the exam papers had to be reread. The instructor protested against this attack on the sanctity of his grades, and in the "Who-shall-guard-the-guardians?" debate that inevitably took place in the Faculty Council, other faculty members insisted that the assigning of grades was solely their responsibility, a "sacred trust," an assistant professor of advertising called it. Herb Mullins had done his homework, however, and now recruited the authority of several registrars from some well-known universities. The grades the faculty submitted were recommendations only — recommendations to him, Herb said — which he then turned into recommendations to the Board of Governors. Never mind that usually all the recommendations were accepted; the ultimate grades belonged to the college, not to individual faculty members.

I remembered this, and wondered now if Herb, as well as being responsible for the students' grades, might also be responsible for the admissions of students, too, even students in the extension program, even for those courses designated "Recreational and Other," even for non-credit courses in Business Communications, even, then, for the Slapshot Boys. As well, I knew that because Herb had the ear of the president he probably knew all about these boys, might even have suggested to the president the route for getting them on the campus and into the hockey team. So I would ask him about them, pass on Simmonds' misery to him, find out, if I could, what we could do about them. Perhaps transfer them to another course, out of my tiny jurisdiction.

"You're just the guy I wanted to see," he had said when I called him from my office. "Some prick in the Personnel department says I shouldn't be writing 'More important' at the beginning of a sentence, but 'More importantly.' But I remember you telling me it should be 'important.' Hang on." There was a short silence while he evidently consulted something on his desk. "Where did that mother go?" he said, to himself. Then, "Ah, adjective, right?"

"It depends. I'll come and see you about it."

"Bring me some coffee. Wanda here won't make it anymore."

"Wanda's become a feminist?"

"No, shit, no. I mean, yes, she's always been her own woman which does include most of the things the feminist crowd stand for, but that's not her problem here. No, she just thinks coffee's bad for me. So come and tell me about 'importantly.'"

Herb and I enjoy one of those rare relationships, nearly friendships, which do not depend on a community of interest, for we have nothing in common except admiration for each other's skills. We had come together at a faculty party, had a conversation about the possibility of a conga line being created and the importance of choosing the best exit to get out of there quickly if we saw that happening. Thereafter we occasionally found ourselves together at a table in the cafeteria. And the more I found myself an outsider to the English department, the more I found myself drinking coffee with Herb Mullins.

Herb's background includes planting tobacco, and working on an oil rig out in Alberta and on an assembly line in the Ford plant in Oshawa. He is a self-educated man, and like all self-educated men he misses the security that the rest of us enjoy when we are faced with a grammatical problem: the security of remembering that none of our teachers at university mentioned the problem, so we are free to confess to an ignorance that isn't our fault. Herb, though, thinks that the university would have taught us everything there is to know about grammar, and the gaps in his knowledge are all his own fault.

He picked me out as someone he could relax with, trust a little; especially someone to whom he could confide his interest in grammar. He started learning grammar quietly, with all the chestnuts; for instance, asking me lightly, apparently in passing, why the sentence "He gave it to John and I" was wrong, and then, over the months, other little problems, like, once, "I read somewhere to avoid the passive voice. What the fuck's the passive voice? Have I got one?"

What was this man doing as the college registrar? Most of the college registrars you meet possess at least a master's degree. They tend to be people, men, most of them, still, who have found they dislike teaching and are not interested in scholarship, but enjoy the cloisters and don't want to leave them, so they become Assistant Directors of Admissions or some such, the lay brothers of the establishment. Herb does not have a graduate degree, nor, for a long time, did he have an undergraduate degree. At some point he enrolled in the extension division of the University of Toronto, and seven years later had a B.A. in Math and Computer Science, and thus, as he explained to me much later, could, at least, "wear a fucking sheepskin around my neck when I'm handing out diplomas."

He owes his appointment to the fact that he is a sort of genius, a near-illiterate with an instinctive and total understanding of computers. Someone in the Philosophy department tried to call him an *idiot savant* but I've looked that up and it's not quite the same thing. A long time ago, perhaps twenty years before, when the college was still small and not sure of itself, when the word "computer" meant a washing machine six feet high and four feet square with a room of its own to stand and hum in, Herb rescued the college from the prospect of a huge fiasco. The administration's computer went down, taking with it the database of student records just days before the year's results were to be printed out. Then the original data — the grades handed in by the departments — disappeared, probably into the garbage. Replacing them in time for graduation was impossible; some of the chairpersons had already left for conferences in Europe or New York or the Greek Islands, taking the keys to the department files with them.

Experts in and out of the college were consulted, but the records remained lost in computer space until someone thought of asking young Herb Mullins, then a lab assistant in the Math department, if he had any suggestions. His chairman brought him into the crisis with a tale of several extraordinary feats Herb had already accomplished, and persuaded the distraught president to let him have a go.

From that day, Herb became a legend. He sat down in front of the computer, polished his fingertips on his shirt like a safe-cracker and caused them to flicker over the keys, like Peter Ustinov in that movie with Maggie Smith. Messages appeared on the screen, and Herb moved along, navigating a route through the messages until after two hours he stood up and said, "You'll be all right now. Just press "Print."

Actually, it must have been more like that movie with Matt Damon playing the janitor/genius.

As he worked, the room behind Herb had steadily filled with administration staff; when the first real message came on the screen, they burst into applause. The president, who had joined the group, now led Herb away to his office and anointed him "Registrar." We were without a registrar at the time, having instead a "Manager of Student Records," and even he had only recently been capitalized as we searched for titles appropriate to our evolving status, so the president didn't have to demote anyone, not that anyone was going to stop him appointing whom he liked. In those days, before committees arrived and the college became set in its ways, the president ran the college by himself. (Later, I became aware that Herb enjoyed a curious relationship with the president who, I'm pretty sure, sought Herb's advice whenever a problem cropped up that was outside the experience of his academic advisors.)

Herb could certainly do the part of the job the president wanted him for, the creating, storing, and printing out of records on demand. But he needed help to carry out some of the other, simpler duties of the registrar. His flaw, a serious one in any institution of higher education, but especially in a newly arrived and status-conscious one like Hambleton, was his grammar, for Herb had retained the vocabulary of the Ford assembly line. However, he soon became aware of his need to sound like a registrar as well as act like one, so he set about improving himself, in case, as he said to me, we ever became a proper college and he a proper registrar. And that was where I came in.

Herb is a quick learner and he found a good secretary, soon managing most of his work without my help, but an occasional new challenge would have him calling me and I would drop by his office to take out an apostrophe or to confirm that the first word after a colon can be capitalized if you want, something that isn't built into the programs of word processors.

Gradually, he learned to trust me. At the time I was just trying to understand computer jargon, having particular trouble at first with the term "default," and after that night at the party he began to help. I was flattered that somebody with his genius treated me as an equal; he, I realized later, was just as pleased to find someone he could talk to about grammar without being betrayed.

Slowly, aided by his secretary, Wanda, Herb has acquired all the ordinary English skills he needs to handle his correspondence, but speaking grammatically is still a strain for him. He manages well enough in public, but it doesn't come naturally, and in private he gets relief by returning to his roots. "Write a letter to this motherfucker. Tell him to stick his money up his ass," he will say to Wanda, giving her a letter from the owner of a furniture store in Sudbury, someone who has offered to contribute to a scholarship fund if we will overlook his son's lack of qualifications for entrance to one of our programs. "Sonofabitch has already had his MPP, the mayor, and his local priest write to us, and now he's into bribing. I wouldn't mind, but apart from being stupid, the kid — kid, Christ, he's twenty-six! — has a record for violence as long as your arm."

Wanda doesn't speak Herb's language, but she watches a lot of those British sitcoms on PBS so she's heard all the language before and she has no problem translating it into polite registrar jargon.

CHAPTER FIVE

ALL THIS IS THE BACKGROUND to my dropping into Herb's office later that morning to see if he could do something about the Slapshot Boys. He was sitting at his desk, his suit jacket hanging on the back of the door, his tie in a noose, neatly knotted and ready to slip over his head, now hanging from the same hook as his jacket.

I also have to take some responsibility for Herb's clothes. When the title of registrar came to him he had spent most of his working life in jeans and a blue leather bomber jacket, but as a registrar he had to dress up. The officers of the college were beginning to find themselves on committees of their fellow registrars in other post-secondary institutions. The first time Herb was invited to join such a committee he came to me for help.

I was puzzled at first: he was wearing a dark suit and a coloured tie, a shirt with French cuffs and heavy gold cufflinks with his initials set in a circle of gold. Like Herb, I hadn't looked at business apparel for twenty years so he looked more or less all right to me, but as he was explaining his problem my eyes cleared and I saw that he wouldn't do. Did anyone on Bay Street wear ties that bright, and cufflinks that big? And weren't the lapels a shade wide?

"This is my wedding suit," Herb said. "I use it for funerals. My wife says it makes me look funny, you know, goofy. So tell me what to get, would you?" He was asking his big brother for help dressing for his first high school dance.

"Moores," I said. "I'll take you downtown to Moores this afternoon." Moores, who sold suits for about a tenth of the price the tailors on Bloor Street charge, was exactly right for Herb, or me if I was ever in his position. "You need two suits, some shirts, a couple of ties, and some brogues."

That afternoon I felt like the Wizard of Oz as I turned Herb into a registrar. In this, as in everything else, he was a quick study. Within a week, after a haircut, he looked like an administrator, although the permanent slightly weathered look he had acquired picking tobacco never completely faded; seeing him for the first time you would guess that he had started life on an oil rig and now had his own drilling company.

Today it seemed to be a good idea to start with Herb's problem, solve it, and then sidle into mine. "About 'importantly,'" I said. "It depends." I sipped my coffee and waited.

"Oh, Christ. Here we fucking go again. Wanda! Listen to this. We're all wrong," he said in a mock show of exasperation. He swivelled back to me. "Why?"

I had had that necessary few seconds to go into lecturing mode. "You're right. Usually it should be 'more important,' adjective, because it's governed by the copula verb."

"Hear that, Wanda? We're okay if the verb is having it off with the noun." He turned back to me, grinning. "And when does this happen?"

"Take the sentence: 'He strutted importantly around the office.' In that case you do need an adverb to modify the verb."

He wrote it down. "I've been making notes. That cocksucker in the Business Section of the *Globe* gets this wrong most of the time."

Herb would notice the *Globe* columnist's error as soon as he learned it himself.

"Herb, be careful. If most people get it wrong, then maybe usage has effected a change since I learned about it. Then it's not wrong."

He thought about that. "But they don't know why they're right, do they? I could still correct them. Upset them a little. Do a little head-fucking."

"Probably."

"Then I'm going to continue to be a stickler for ... what?"

"Tradition. You could be against modishness."

"I'll do that. There's nothing in Fowler, you know." Herb loves Fowler.

"That cuts the risk."

He made a note and put the letter aside. "So. What can I do for you?"

"The Slapshot Boys. The boys you and the president brought in to play hockey. Remember?"

Herb grinned. I didn't have to identify them further.

"They're causing problems for one of my instructors."

"But not to the president. Our team lost to Brock 7-5 last Tuesday. That's the best result we've had in two years. Those clowns scored two each."

"And put one of the Brock team in hospital."

"Yeah, that helped. Who is this instructor? What's his problem? Maybe he doesn't belong here."

"Simmonds. David Simmonds. New this semester, but there are no complaints about him so far. As I understand it, these two guys are right off the map — illiterate, swearing in class — not aggressive, you understand — that's just the way they grew up."

"Disruptive, eh? Simmonds? Simmonds?" he repeated as if he recognized the name. "Is this guy afraid of them?"

It hadn't occurred to me. "I don't think so, no. He would kick them out himself if we gave him the okay."

Later, I realized that I should have noticed that there was something not quite right about Herb's response. He seemed slightly amused, yet wondering, as if he were intrigued by my judgment of this unknown instructor. He said, "So has, er, Simmonds sent them to you to deal with? Like, er, sending them to the principal?" He grinned again.

"To me? Herb, have you seen these guys? I don't know about Simmonds but I'm afraid of them."

"Send them along to me, then. They've got to stay registered until we win something or the win won't count. Maybe I can talk their language. Where else can we put them?"

"I thought of Public Speaking 101."

"You're in a real twist, aren't you?" He picked a calendar off a shelf behind him and flicked through it. "'Life Writing.' What's that?"

"Sort of writing your memoir, your life story."

"These Slapshot Boys would have a new slant on that, wouldn't they? Listen to this." Herb read, in a prissy voice, "'Everyone has an interesting story to tell — their own. This is an opportunity to get your story down, have it listened to, and get help to make it come alive as narrative. No previous experience required.'" He continued in his normal voice, "Sounds possible, don't you think? These guys must have some lively experiences to tell, as soon as they learn to write. Tell you what, I'll talk to the instructor, see if he'll take them." He changed the topic. "How's it with you, these days?" Herb knows my situation.

"The same. The part-timers just got this year's reminder from the dean that our contracts expire in May."

"You knew that already. Why is he saying it again?"

"Our lawyer says it's probably what their lawyer has advised them to do. By sending this letter the administration is *ipso facto* ending any previous understanding, and if I want to protest I have to do it now."

"*Ipso facto*," eh?" He rolled his eyes, enjoying the fancy phrase. "That right? So? You going to hire a lawyer?"

"I got one of these letters last year, and the year before, so I should have protested before this. Not having done so, they would say, is an act of tacit agreement."

"Would they, though? What's the plan, then?"

"I'll find another job, I guess. Carole's due soon. I don't want to be out of work when it arrives. The labour market in Canada is buoyant, I hear." I tried to speak lightly. Although I wanted to share my problem, I recoiled from seeming to cast myself as potentially destitute, wandering Toronto looking for shelter, a newborn babe in my arms. It wasn't that tragic. We could live on Carole's salary until I found some sort of job.

Herb had never made a comment on Carole's pregnancy. I had told him early, but we never talked about it. He had no children, I knew, but I didn't know why and he didn't encourage me to ask. "Have you tried out for a high school?" he said now.

"I'm too old. I'm forty. Anyway, all the high school teachers I've met work too hard. One I know prepares classes four nights a week and all day Sunday. Then there are the parents, the ones who want you to realize what damage you're doing by giving their kid the grade he deserves. One teacher I know was threatened by a parent with a lawsuit if he didn't give his son an A so he could get into med school. The parent was a lawyer."

"Yeah?" Herb was fascinated. "Did he give him the A?"

"He didn't, but his principal did. No, high school is out. The teachers lack support, as they say."

"And there's no hope of a teaching job around here? How come we hired you?"

"When I came, the college needed someone at the last minute. You were desperate. I mean the college was. You aren't now. Even if you were, you wouldn't take me. I don't have a Ph.D."

"How about the teaching? That count? You get pretty good response from the students, don't you, on those assessments?"

"Good enough. They gave me all A's and B's last year, except for one little bastard who gave me an F. There's one of those every year. Anyway, I don't speak the new languages — *deconstruction*, *structuralism*, *post-structuralism* — so I'd never get through the interviews."

"Does everybody else in your department speak this stuff?"

"Not the old ones, but they don't have to; they've got tenure. But you can't get a job without knowing something about these new criticisms and learning new criticisms is a young man's game. It's too late for me. I'm a dodo."

"Do you like it? Teaching, I mean."

"Yes. Yes, I do like it. I like showing them how a poem or a novel works. Some days I just want to jump off a cliff but mostly I go home happy. It's about ninety percent ego satisfaction, of course, but I feel I'm doing something ...," I searched for the right word, "... worth paying me for."

He brought the front legs of his chair crashing to the floor. "To a guy like me, it could sound like a bunch of bullshit, about as useful as doing crossword puzzles. Anyway, poems, short stories, long stories — how will they help them make a living?"

He was winding me up, trying to get me to talk about the importance of culture and art. He's done it before. "They won't," I said. "But the students don't realize that until they graduate. They aren't as sharp as you."

He laughed. "Okay, but seriously, would you tell me one day why they should be studying stuff like this when they could be learning something useful? We're supposed to be a bilingual country! Tell me, does anyone in the English department speak French?"

"Some. A little. But none of them is bilingual. It's changing, though. Those immersion programs are working, I hear."

"I'll bet the faculty at the University of Montreal all speak English, wouldn't you say?"

You have to put up with Herb when he's on a rant. He was wound up now. He continued, "Did you see that article in the paper last week, by some local professor? About what's wrong with the universities in this province? You know, we are underfunded, the high schools aren't doing their job, there are too many students in university these days — all the usual stuff ..."

"I didn't see it, no. But there's one of those articles every six months or so."

"That's my impression, too. I always read them, see what you guys are thinking. You know something? I've never seen one that blamed the professors for what's wrong with the universities."

"We're the ones who write the articles."

"Ain't it the truth? So send the Slapshot Boys along. How about this instructor of yours? Maybe he's the problem. Is he new?"

"Yes, but I think these so-called students are the problem. Let's try them with 'Life Writing.'"

"But he's doing okay, right?" Herb persisted. "This new guy?"

"Nobody's complaining. None of his other students, I mean."

"You would have heard from them, right, if this guy was a kook?"

"By now, yes."

Later, I realized that Herb's interest in Simmonds should have caught my attention, but at the time I had only the Slapshot Boys in mind and it went right by me.

Back in my office, I continued to look for something to take my mind off Carole. It arrived in the form of a phone call from Jack Chuval, the chairman of the English department. "Have you seen *The Rag*?" he shouted. "No? Read it. Tell me who wrote it." He hung up.

The Rag is Hambleton's radical student newspaper. The other student paper, *The Hambletonian*, is a creature of the Journalism department.

Jack's concern with *The Rag* was about a two-page article starting on page 3, headed "Understanding Mammon," that attacked the pitch the university is currently making to create an M.B.A. program in competition with three other graduate business schools already servicing the community.

The article began by rehearsing the familiar complaints about the amoral, even wicked ways of the business world, and listed half a dozen recent examples of the corruption endemic in big business. "We live in a culture of greed," the author wrote, as if he had just thought of it, and then summarized the arguments against Hambleton's having an M.B.A. program. These were familiar, too. The arguments were: first, it wasn't necessary because most of today's tycoons had managed to stay out of jail without M.B.A.'s; second, only the rich could afford the fees of an M.B.A. program and therefore, third, it's sole function was to make the rich richer, hardly a proper role for a university.

There followed some chat about the idea of a university, bringing in all the usual people — Arnold, Newman, Plato — and then the writer moved on to asking, since this was all obvious, why is another M.B.A. program being contemplated? The answer, he said, lay in the ambitions of presidents and deans who are already under the spell cast by the business world that bigger is better, that an administrator is important by virtue of the size of what he administers.

The article was signed, "An English Instructor," which made it slightly embarrassing for Jack, and, I suppose, for the rest of us.

The phone rang. It was Chairman Jack Cheval again. "Who wrote it?" he demanded to know. He was very angry.

"I don't know, Jack. One of your colleagues, it says."

Jack said, "Listen: there will be a reply in the next edition, an article signed by fourteen Business instructors and the dean. The article will be full of phrases like "planning for the future" (a favourite pleonasm in business education) and the usual cracks about the uselessness of teaching poetry to students whose command of ordinary English is so poor they can't write a decent business letter. I hope that will be all, that by then we will have shut up the asshole in our department who wrote the article before he enrages the whole college. English Literature, including the reading of poetry, has survived as part of the curriculum even in some of the programs designed for what the Business division calls the "real world," only because our opponents are diffident. These people have felt intimidated all their lives by literature and its teachers, but it's my feeling that times have changed, that if this letter-writing moron keeps on, the business people will gather up their courage and put together arguments to get rid of us entirely. It's been done in other places. Our survival at Hambleton has depended on their reluctance to take up arms, but I think they might do something after an article like this. The president is going ape. He hasn't got the provincial funding for the business school yet. Find this bastard, Joe, and quick." He hung up.

It was a good speech and obviously carefully worked out, perhaps prepared for the next closed meeting of the English department. I found myself looking in the mirror, asking it why I should concern myself with Jack Cheval's problems, since he was apparently so relaxed about mine. The answer came back that there was no point in burning bridges yet. Perhaps the entire English department would come down with West Nile Virus as the result of going to their annual picnic on Centre Island, and I would be the only healthy instructor available, for a while. That would do for now, but the fact that I was even asking the question showed how far I had come along the road towards telling them all to go fuck themselves. For fifteen years now I had been living a hand-to-mouth existence and in that time not one of my full-time colleagues had lifted a finger to protest my situation. Some of them looked embarrassed when the issue arose, but mainly they just looked away.

Now, I said, "Jack, I think you're panicking. These arguments are clichés now, given the stench that's coming off Wall Street. Relax."

Two days later *The Rag* published a reply. A banner on the front page displayed the line, "Let Me Count the Ways," with the instruction to see page 3. On page 3, the line was repeated followed by the subheading, "A reply to an English instructor by a Business instructor."

It began with a reference to the English instructor's little polemic, complimenting the writer on the wit and elegance of his prose, and then moving to wondering "if the writer felt entirely comfortable, as an English instructor, in attacking another discipline on campus, even on a campus like Hambleton."

Then there was some entertaining chat about the "never-never land" of English literary criticism. (He had great fun with archetypal criticism, telling us he had heard it described, by an English professor on another campus, as a "profundity machine": you put "Mary Had a Little Lamb" in at one end and profundity comes out of the other.) As for the latest critical theories (he got some amusement out of five or six fashionable schools of criticism, including one that sounded as if he had made it up), they reminded him of what he had heard of medieval theologians commenting on the Bible, especially the kind that sought to find the key to crack the code the text must embed; call them the cabalists? No doubt it was all pretty harmless. Or was it? Should we condone the apparent growing tendency to fragmentation in English studies, the drive to make specialists of the students before they can read and write? A recent examination put out by the English department contained twenty-seven questions.

The course was taught by three instructors, and each instructor had contributed nine questions of which the students had to answer four. What the student had to do first was identify which nine had been put on the paper by his own instructor. This was not as difficult as it sounded, because the other eighteen questions would be completely unintelligible to him. That, the writer said, is what the teaching of literature has come to. Could even the instructors have answered their colleagues' questions? he asked.

All true, of course, and it doesn't matter that it's all been said before, usually at greater length, and mainly by members of English departments attacking each other. It will look like original thought to our enemies on the Hambleton campus.

But the real question it posed was, who wrote it? Because it would reflect well on the Business department that a member of their faculty was familiar enough with the latest fads in literary criticism to have written about them so comfortably. Some of the sub-topics referred to — "Gender Studies" and "Queer Studies," for instance — were even outside the experience of many members of the English department, such is the range of critical positions that have emerged over the last thirty years. But this bird seemed too much at home referring to these new pockets of thought for even the most erudite instructor of Business.

The phone rang. It was Jack, our chairman. "You found the sonofabitch?" he shouted.

I said, "The obvious conclusion, if you've read any spy fiction, is that we have a mole — that this letter was written by a member of our own department seeking to sabotage us. But that is simply to assume that a pattern familiar elsewhere would make sense here, and it doesn't. The idea of a member of our English department secretly recruited into the cause of business is surely unthinkable. Don't you agree? A more likely idea is that a member of the Business department is smart enough to have consulted someone off campus."

"Never mind the mole bullshit. Do you have any idea who wrote the thing? You know the editor of this paper — Toft?

"I know who he is."

"Could you find out from him?"

"Why me, Jack?"

"Aren't you some kind of Dick Tracy? All right then, you because I doubt if you wrote it, and if you find out, then, well, you're a bit of an outsider when I come to handle it. See?"

He was having trouble with his words, but one was enough — "outsider."

"Are there brownie points in it for me?" I asked.

"Go and see Toft," he said. Then, "Joe, this is just an errand. Don't get your hopes up."

He's honest, our Jack: he can't find work that isn't there. So for the time being, I stayed civil.

JASON TOFT WAS A THIN, pale-faced Scot in his mid-twenties with black hair parted in the middle, projecting, badly stained teeth, and a nose that sprouted a number of what in a much older man would be called grog blossoms, encouraged to bloom in Toft's case by his habitual nose-picking. He personified for me the word *ferret*, though I had never seen one.

The office of *The Rag* is housed in the basement of an old building the college appropriated twenty years ago and never found another use for. I found Toft standing outside the front door, smoking and reading an old *New Yorker*, which he stuffed into his pocket as I approached. Whenever Toft wasn't actually writing or on the phone, he conducted the paper's business in the open air, even at twenty below, so that he could smoke.

I introduced myself. "You've caused quite a fuss in the administration with this feud you're stirring up," I said. "I'm here from the president to ask you to stop it. Now. It's an entertaining debate, but that's enough."

I didn't really expect Toft to fall in line and revert to a respectful fifties-type student. I was just trying to nudge him off balance. I'd done my homework on Toft. He came to Canada with a good degree from Glasgow, wanting a job in journalism. He was openly contemptuous of our program, and had hoped to avoid having to enrol in it by getting a job on a Canadian newspaper with his Classics degree, but he had found that now that Journalism degrees and diplomas are being offered at a dozen colleges and universities in the province, the media generally expected all new applicants to have one.

Our Journalism program is not arduous for someone of Toft's background and ability, and he had found himself with a lot of time on his hands, time that he filled by working at *The Rag*. Three months after he arrived he had taken over the running of the paper and had got it to the point where the senior administrators and many of the faculty opened each new issue uneasily.

He sneered. He looked around to make sure his assistant editors were lurking in the doorway within earshot. "Is tha' an orrrder?" he asked, loudly.

I switched tactics, and became man-to-man. I said, "Don't be an asshole, Jason, and don't take me for one. Of course it's not an order. The president can't tell you how to run the paper, unless you offend the standards of the community."

"And how would I go abou' tha'?"

"Oh, you know, cartoons of administration figures doing indelicate things to each other, rude remarks about the Governor General, stuff like that. No, it's a request, a warning from one responsible administrator to another, a warning of what will happen if you go too far."

"What you would do, you mean?"

"Me? I'm just a messenger. I don't give a fuck. No, what the president would do. What the community might demand. But you know all that. There's a course on it in your program, isn't there? Called 'Free Speech: Rights and Responsibilities.'"

"We do have responsibilities. Does Bluebell realize tha'?" ("Bluebell" is the students' nickname for the president. He got his nickname because of a little sailing boat he keeps in the Toronto harbour. His real name is Malcolm Campbell and he christened his boat *Bluebird*, the same name the famous Sir Malcolm gave to *his* boat and car. When *The Rag* found out about the sailing boat they renamed the man on the spot, changing "Bluebird" to "Bluebell" because it sounded even sillier. There was a time when the president could have expelled the lot of them for something like that, but today he just has to put up with it.)

"Of course he does. Yon president's no' a bluidy fool." And there I was at it again, an old tic of mine, imitating and therefore seeming to make fun of someone's accent. I watched Toft's face harden into that of an enemy. "Look," I said, hurriedly, "I just came by to pass on a friendly warning that a note of alarm has been sounded upstairs. You might tell the wits on the faculty who are writing this stuff that it is clever, but it is also a bit cowardly not to sign their names. I assume you know who they are and are offering them protection?"

"You think it's the faculty?"

"He says he is, or they do, if it's a pair. And the prose seems typical of the faculty."

"Is that what you think? It couldna' be someone doing a clever imitation of the faculty? Hiding behind the pseudonym, so to speak?"

"Anything's possible, of course. Anyway, I wouldn't print any more."

I got out then. I didn't want to get into a slanging match with someone who had probably once been president of the Glasgow

Speakers' Union and majored in Demosthenes. Whatever harm I had done, I had also, I hoped, accomplished something of what I set out to do: planted a seed of doubt, made him wobble a little. My feeling from this very brief encounter was that Toft was someone to deal with at arm's length, preferably by mail. To borrow a phrase I had read somewhere, he was not the kind of ferret you would keep in your trousers.

CHAPTER SIX

I HAD FOUND ALL THIS — Simmonds' problems with the Slapshot Boys, anonymous articles in *The Rag*, grooming Herb Mullins, Vladimir's antics in the parking lot — no more than welcome distractions from my preoccupation with Carole's pregnancy. Most of the time I couldn't think about it to any purpose, and at the same time I couldn't think about anything else. Carole, on the other hand, continued to refuse to be anything but pleased with herself. I didn't know how we would cope, especially financially, and I was very worried. She, apparently, wasn't. An early episode will illustrate.

No more than a month after she had revealed her condition, I found her in the cheese section of Loblaws, trying to make up her mind between Romano and Parmesan. A month before, to Carole, grated cheese was anything you sprinkled on broccoli to make it edible; she knew nothing about varieties. And both of us only ate broccoli to keep scurvy at bay.

I said, "This is what we've run out of," holding up a canister of Kraft.

"Freshly grated is what we want. This is it." She handed me what felt and looked like a piece of an old stone wall. It was Romano, fifteen dollars the piece, about a quarter of a pound.

I said, "We'll need a new pepper grinder, too, then, one about four feet long in a cradle, on wheels. One we can trundle around the table when guests come."

She smiled. "Don't be silly." She consulted a list. "Balsamic vinegar, chilies, chicken pieces for curry. Here. Hold this." She handed me a stick of bread.

I looked around for the cart.

"Right behind you."

I had noticed it but passed it by, because it looked like the cart of someone shopping for a dinner party for twenty people, filled to the brim with expensive-looking delicatessen-type groceries. The little space in front of the handle usually reserved by me for soft, unboxed cake was full of books, two large ones and one small — a Jamie Oliver (the Italian one); *The Cuisine of the Sun*, by Mirielle Johnston; and Julia Child's *The Art of French Cooking*. About this last, I said, "I think I've seen this before."

"It's just been reissued."

I forbore to point out that she had not opened the first edition more than twice in three years. It was all very weird, but I didn't say a word.

The total, when we got to the checkout, was two hundred and thirty dollars, about three times our normal weekly grocery bill. I waited in vain for her to squeal. (She is not cheap; she just used to resent spending money on anything but books and films. Not now, apparently.)

At home, while I unpacked — we had carried in eight bags — Carole cracked some eggs, made an omelette, tossed a salad, opened a bottle of white wine we'd had for six months because white wine normally gave her mouth ulcers, removed the carefully warmed bread from the oven, and we sat down to a feast. All this from someone who had hitherto taken no more pleasure in her kitchen than I take in my tool box.

"Now I know you're pregnant. Is this permanent, this new cuisine?"

"I just felt like doing some cooking."

"So you said before. I never thought I'd live to hear you utter those words. And shouldn't we be economizing?" I asked.

"Savour the moment. It may be a temporary phase. How do I know?" she said. "Pregnant women do experience overwhelming needs — sardines, chocolate milk, stuff like that. I have a need to cook, rare in me, as you know. I'll cash in my RRSPs if we have to."

"You going to bake, too? Apple pan dowdy, upside-down cake, meat loaf, stuff like that?"

"I doubt it. Not now you've noticed. I can feel it wearing off."

I thought carefully about my next words, finally choosing the obvious ones. I said, "Carole" (for emphasis — there was no one else in the room), "it's been on my mind to ask. You must have known for a month before you said anything. Why didn't you say something before?"

"I wanted to be sure and I might as well tell you. It isn't a complete accident. I got sick of chemically engineering my reproductive system so I thought I'd try the Catholic method. It didn't work."

There was no need to say any more. Besides, I realized that the best response for a compulsive talker, the response that would show how seriously I was taking this news, was silence.

AT BREAKFAST THE NEXT MORNING (still eight months ago), we were already nearly back to normal. We had not eaten breakfast together since those first few wonderful mornings of our relationship when we were feeling each other out, establishing quickly that both of us preferred to eat breakfast — toast and coffee, that is — alone with a book or *The Globe and Mail.* After the first week, if we happened to coincide, we ignored each other until we were nearly ready to leave the house.

When I sat down, she said, "What do Winnipeggers eat for breakfast: Pancakes? Grits? Black pudding?"

She was feeling larky, of course, or, perhaps, in view of the serious mood of the previous evening, sardonic, as she wound down from her "hormonal" episode. I had never eaten black pudding in my life, although I knew what it was from English novels. She knew that. I left Winnipeg twenty years ago having been happy there in my salad days (when I was just learning to eat the stuff — salad, I mean) but glad to be moving on. And I have never spoken yearningly of those days or of the cuisine of a Winnipeg WASP. Even my taste for cabbage rolls and sour cream, which I had acquired at the house of a Ukranian girlfriend, I had managed to leave behind.

"It used to be coffee and donuts," I said. "Now it's probably croissants like everybody else."

She smiled. "I forgot to buy coffee. Will tea do, until you get to Starbucks?"

I was used to her pregnancy now, and everything that happened was framed within the awareness that I would have to make some changes soon. One of the few rules I live by is, "When in doubt, do nothing," but it looked as if it wasn't safe to live by it much longer.

A WEEK AFTER VLADIMIR PETROV's car went missing, Tommy Stokoe was waiting at the parking lot gate again, holding up his hand.

"Who'd they get this time, Tommy?" I left my engine running.

"Woman in Journalism," he told my rear tire. "She's ditzy but not as bad as Petrov. She's sure she drove it to work but it was gone when she went home I mean if they want these lots to be secure they're going to have to give me more guards I can't do it with what I've got."

"Christ! You mean a car was stolen?"

"Last night a new Subaru she said ..."

"Did they break the lock on the gate?" Everyone had by now been issued fresh cards with which to operate the new gate that had been installed.

"She kept the card in her glove compartment all they had to do was get in the car which for these cowboys would be easy I'll have to put in another system one that records who is operating the gate I asked for one but they said it was too expensive cheaper than being sued by someone owning a goddamn Subaru wouldn't you think anyway I was just letting you know you are going to have to get another card as soon as the system's in place in the meantime I've got temporary guards on all the lots until midnight after that if some airhead like Petrov forgets he's on his own but we'll be okay when the new system comes in two days probably."

One day, I thought, I will secretly tape one of your monologues and use it as a sight exercise in punctuation. Or maybe break it up into fragments and set it out as verse, title it "At the Gate," send it to a little magazine.

Finally somebody pulled up behind me and I escaped.

TOMMY STOKOE CAME BY AGAIN in the early afternoon while I was preparing a class on "You Touched Me" for the tenth or fifteenth time. As an undergraduate, I shared the conventional disdain we had for professors who lectured us from the same yellowing notes year after year, so now I have my notes on disc and I print up a fresh-looking set every time I use them. The fact is, like any teacher, I am at my best when I know my topic backwards. In English, that isn't easy. The problem is that just as you think you've got a handle on

King Lear and are looking forward to next year so you can use your new insight while discovering others, they change the course and you have to wrestle with *As You Like It*, which you've never found a way to make riveting to students in Social Work.

For a long time, Lawrence, for me, was *Sons and Lovers* and a handful of novels that were easy to put down, in every sense. I found a lack of ordinariness in these novels; I found them overburdened with the joys of sex. Then came (to me) *England Their England*, twelve stories by a Lawrence I had never met. All twelve were exciting discoveries, but one of them, "You Touched Me," I look forward to teaching whenever I get the chance.

I was just putting fresh Sellotape on some of the pages of my Penguin edition when Tommy Stokoe interrupted me to present me with the new parking lot key.

"Already?" I asked. "When does it become effective?"

"As of now in security you have to jump ahead of these guys you know get your lock changed when you've been broken into so the companies are ready to act right away after an incident ..."

"So how will it work? I mean, any differently?"

"There's a little computer in the new gatepost that records every card and who owns it."

"That should help. You'll know who the thief is if he's on staff."

"We figured the last one was using a stolen card maybe one of the women who lost a card in the washroom then got it replaced this time if he does it again we'll have a better lead." He shifted his gaze from the floor to the window, then straightened up.

"You going to distribute those today?" I asked him. It looked like a big job, finding a couple of hundred people in their offices on a single afternoon.

"We'll do most of them at the gate over the next couple days I just came by thought you'd be interested how's that new guy making out?"

"What!" What, indeed. What the hell did Tommy Stokoe care about the "new guy"?

"That guy Simmonds how's he doing?"

"He's okay. Why? You think he's been stealing cars?"

"I just wondered how he's making out."

He left me slightly wondering about this new camaraderie that had sprung up between us. Maybe he was assessing my potential as a security guard. It was no secret on the campus that the part-timers on the faculty were steadily being cut adrift.

And then I had a real problem to deal with: Simmonds again.

At seven-fifteen, a head poked itself around my office door, a blond, middle-aged, female head, about fifty, I guessed, attractive if a bit highly coloured around the cheekbones and with a small double chin. "Excuse me, sir." She rapped sharply on her side of the door. "Mr. Simmonds has not appeared to teach us. Ought we to wait?" Correct syntax with a slight mid-European accent.

If something had happened to Simmonds, the department secretary, Myfanwy, would have left me a note. I had been out to get something to eat at a good Kurdish café nearby where you can get a tasty plate of Persian meatballs and rice for seven dollars and I had not noticed any message before I left. Now I looked harder and found it, tucked into the corner of my blotter, just, "Mr. Simmonds will not be in tonight."

I promised myself a chat with Simmonds as soon as he appeared, but in the meantime I said, to the student, "I think something might have happened to delay him. Would you tell the class that Mr. Simmonds or someone else will be along in five minutes, please? Me, probably."

That is, me, the person in charge of English non-credit courses at night. Night school students, especially those without any previous college experience, are likely to assume that the person in charge of the department was promoted on ability, and that in getting me they would be getting the best.

But this one looked unimpressed. "Mr. Simmonds was going to teach 'The Letter of Complaint' tonight. We are prepared for that."

"I don't want to do anything to interfere with Mr. Simmonds' plans. Has he taught any classes on punctuation yet?"

"It is Correspondence for Business we are studying," she said.

"I know, but even in business you should be able to punctuate. I expect Mr. Simmonds planned to teach it later on. I'll introduce the topic tonight."

She looked doubtful. "You do not usually teach Business Correspondence?"

A piece of near-impertinence but maybe she had had some bad experiences. I said, coldly, "I just don't want to interfere with Mr. Simmonds' plans. I'll be along in a moment."

I was more pleased than not. I took out a file I had had for eight years. One of the sets of notes in the file was headed "The Ten Uses of the Comma." It was a chapter in a projected grammar text that I started to write when I first began teaching English in night school, an idea to make my fortune, called *Grammar for Grown-Ups*. It never got off the ground, but this chapter had done me service several times since then, and I keep it in my drawer with a full set of exercises for emergencies like this.

Tonight thirty students had been waiting since seven o'clock for their class to begin. If this happens during the regular day programs, or rather, when it happens during the regular day programs (for after the first week of term not many days go by in the Faculty of Arts without it happening), you just cancel the class. The instructor phones to say he's so ill he can barely hold the phone, the department secretary announces that Professor So-and-So has the glotch, and asks someone who is teaching near So-and-So's classroom to tell the students.

The students accept this for about a week, after which they conclude that Professor So-and-So's illness is interfering with their education and begin to ask when he is to be replaced. Night school students, though, have often put in a hard day's graft in offices and warehouses, some of them twenty miles out of the city, and they have travelled in the dead of a Toronto winter or in a sweltering heat wave for an hour in order to improve themselves. They don't want to hear about cancellations, only about replacements.

Simmonds' students were evidently satisfied with him. The response at the beginning of the class when I explained the situation showed that; there was no huge collective moan of disappointment, but no sigh of relief, either.

I began, as I always do with these sure-win classes, with a trick. I wrote ten sentences on the board and asked them to copy them out and put in the commas. Each sentence contained an example of one of the ten uses of the comma. Then, when they were all finished, I got them to exchange their papers with the person in the next row. Then we set about correcting them. I don't give a detailed explanation of each error and correction at this stage. The object is to provide each student with a list of his own errors. Thus when we had them corrected I gathered them up and redistributed them to their authors.

Now I distributed a further set of exercises, more examples of the ten rules I had started with, and these we did together. This time, I told them not to mark up the exercise until we had the correct solution, so that they would finish up with a set of examples they could keep for reference.

All this takes a lot of time, which is part of its value. What with the break, we didn't get past Use Number Three in the second set of examples. I told them that if Mr. Simmonds didn't appear, I or someone else would take over next week, and, in further preparation, off the top of my head, I told them I wanted them all to bring a question, real or fake, about the use of the apostrophe. This is not really a suitable gimmick for night school students, who don't get a chance to find out from each other in the cafeteria what I've been talking about for the last hour, but I was trying to scrape together a second lecture to prepare myself for the possibility that Simmonds had had an accident and would be gone for the rest of the term. Besides, punctuation had recently become trendy as at least two journalists had written best-sellers on the topic, so my students would have no trouble cribbing interesting examples.

I had seen the Slapshot Boys as soon as I walked in, sitting at the back in the corner. Their faces were raw and scuffed with the marks of their trade. The classroom is fitted with chairs with one arm big enough to take notes on, and within ten minutes one of them had arranged himself for sleep on the arm of his chair. The other tried to look like a student, sitting up, pencil in hand, staring at me. Whenever he guessed I had made a point, he nodded vigorously and made some marks in an exercise book he had brought with him. When I distributed the sentences to be corrected, he made a show of putting in the commas, then, sometimes, rubbing them out and putting them somewhere else. All the while his teammate slept.

At the break, the wide-awake one nudged his mate upright, and they left. They didn't return after the break, so I never saw where the alert one had put his commas. When the class resumed, there was a slightly sniggering air in the room as the students waited, I think, for me to make some comment, but I continued the lesson briskly, and let them think what they liked. If I should continue to teach the class, and if the Slapshot Boys returned, I needed a strategy to handle them and I hadn't thought of one yet, so it was much too soon to be complicit in the class's amusement, and thus encourage it. Better to be thought humourless by the class than risk the reaction of the Slapshot Boys if they caught me laughing at them.

CHAPTER SEVEN

THE RAG USUALLY PUBLISHES ONCE a week, but Toft had judged that "this was a matter of such interest as to warrant a special supplement." I was surprised because I thought the two previous letters had said it all, but, of course, Toft had the limelight now, and he was loving it.

The new letter (from the "English Instructor") began by defending the twenty-seven question exam that the "Business Instructor" had made fun of, insisting that it was an understandable consequence of the explosion of knowledge in the discipline. Surely soon, the writer said, this knowledge explosion, like all others, will be followed by an ordering and a formalizing of the fresh ideas, and then a sharing of the consequences, to create a new commonality of understanding. Now is not the time, the writer said, to impose restraints on the growth of knowledge, to limit instructors in what they are allowed to think and teach, and students in what they might learn.

All this was no more than rhetorical throat-clearing.

A couple more paragraphs followed, this time written in the kind of language supreme courts use when they are justifying their choice of president — verbose, cloudy, and trying to score new points with old figures (avoiding "procrustean bed" but only just). Then the writer moved on to the questions of exams in general, and here the prose improved as he came to his subject. The bottom line, he said, is that at least the English department, along with the History, Philosophy, and Political Science departments, still expected students to write in sentences, thus giving them a bit of practice for when they joined what the business community called "the real world," whereas a casual survey of the exams of the Business department reveals that most of the questions are of the Yes/No type, to be responded to by ticking a box, the answers to be recorded by a computer. Thus, the student might spend four years in business school, clinging to whatever language skills he acquired in high school, but find himself unable to meet the demands of his employment. That is why the actual business world as opposed to the "real" one is obliged to contract out any writing and editing they need to graduates of English working as freelancers.

Now he moved on to new ground with some familiar points about the morality of the business world. He understood, for instance, that the instructors in Retailing (I) routinely advise those of their students who are planning to open a shop to pay their suppliers last — if possible, only when they have sold the goods they have ordered. That way, the supplier risked bankruptcy before the retailer.

"Is this ethical?" the writer asked. "What about the wholesaler? No doubt there is similar advice for him in Retailing (II), telling the students interested in wholesaling to stick the manufacturer with the red ink they should have incurred themselves."

Now the writer moved to what medievalists would call the argument from authority. The richest man in the world had recently called for an increased number of technologists to be trained, people who could lead us into the new age. He had not called for an increased number of M.B.A.'s, a telling omission, thus raising the question, do we need more Business graduates, and post-graduates? In what way is a shortage (if one exists) of Business graduates holding us back? What is a shortage of Business graduates? How big is the shortage?

Now the writer came back to the old chestnut, that many of our most successful tycoons have no formal Business education. The only reason that the business world prefers to hire Business graduates is that it saves companies the trouble of giving new employees training in the language of the world they are entering, the elementary vocabularies of economics, accounting, and the stock and commodity markets. The employers take the M.B.A. as a sign that recruits have the basic skills necessary to read the Business section of the *Globe*, though they could teach their new employees such skills in a few weeks on the job.

For what is this activity called "business"? First, it isn't Industry, with which it is often linked. The world of Industry is a genuine one, requiring its workers to know something about all sorts of things, chiefly the techniques of manufacturing, and about materials, and about technology. Industry needs engineers, not M.B.A.'s. But what the Business graduate needs to know is how to buy cheap and sell dear and not to have too much left for the January sales. That is all. For the retailer and wholesaler most of what is professed in Business schools is just chat, and easily gained on the job. The function of Industry is to make the goods the community needs; the function of business is to make money. So should the taxpayer subsidize the training of Business students?

There was much more: the editor had allowed him a full two pages, but throughout you could feel the writer licking his lips as he moved towards the clincher, as he employed the familiar dodge of bewailing the lack of space in order to "go directly" to his last point, which was, "What is it about business that requires six or eight years of study? As Dr. Johnson said in advising a widow to continue her dead husband's printing business, 'If business were difficult, those who do it, could not,'" — a crack guaranteed to enrage everyone in the "real world," not just the Business department.

Something in this tugged at me. It was the memory of Toft tucking away *The New Yorker* when I appeared at the newspaper's office. I recognized the cover of the issue and made a mental note to look it up. There was some connection here with the debate in *The Rag*, and I dragged the two references to the top of my mind to sit there as I waited for them to link up. I know better than to rush something like this. Recently I had reread a lot of Wordsworth and Hopkins, hunting for the phrase, "lonely on fell as chat" until my erudite friend, Boris of York, told me it was from Auden, which I might have guessed, old Wystan being master of the fake.

The phone rang. It was my chairman, asking me to come to his office right away.

"Close the door," he said, when I arrived. "Once more, tell me who you think wrote this," he waved a copy of *The Rag*. "And the one the other day."

He was very disgruntled. He took the job of chairman mainly because if he does it for seven years, his pension will be based on his chairman's salary, but also because the faculty asked him to. Jack Cheval belongs to none of the factions in the department; he is mildly interested in most of the new movements but skeptical of the importance of any of them. He has a Ph.D. in Anglo-Saxon, a language not spoken at Hambleton, though Jack raises the possibility of a course "in my area" every year at the annual first meeting of the curriculum committee. We don't take him seriously. Who would teach the course if Jack got sick? Mollified by this sort-of-compliment, Jack smiles and says, "Ah, yes, traditional learning is dead here, like everywhere else," and someone catcalls jocularly, "How's your Greek, Jack?" and we move on. I think the study of Anglo-Saxon has made him sweet-tempered. He presides over the prickliest of department meetings, reducing the level of passion, urging us to be accommodating, always working on the principle that there's no principle that can't be set aside if there's a bus to catch. In the old days when the department was interviewing a candidate for a new position, the members of the committee had to keep in mind all the kinds of prejudice they could be accused of if they turned the candidate down. As chairman, Jack gave the committee a huge advantage, because he's black, from Trinidad, and has a Cambridge degree — a very, very difficult man for a candidate to accuse of bias.

I said, "Why are you asking me, Jack? I might have written it myself."

He said, "Given your political views and your doubtful morals, then, yes, you might have. It crossed my mind. But then I saw this." He read a few sentences of the latest letter. "Now that might have been written by Eustace Tilley. Not by you, anyway. Besides, as an administrator now, however minor, you would feel uneasy attacking the establishment, wouldn't you? So who wrote it?"

None of the personal stuff was intended to be taken seriously. He himself lives with a woman twenty years older than he, an Icelandic scholar at the downtown university. But he had inadvertently raised another question, one much more important to me than identifying the letter writer. I said, "Hold on a minute, Jack. Are you asking me because I have a job on the side, sometimes involving looking for missing persons, which you think gives me some kind of expertise in tracking down anonymous letter writers?"

"Maybe your boss at the detective agency would have some ideas?"

"And if we — me and my boss — find this character, will it make any difference?"

"Of course. I'll reprimand the bugger at least. Unprofessional conduct."

I took my time responding. "Me, Jack, me. Will it help me?"

Now he heard me. "Everybody will be pleased," he said. "All the way up to the president."

"Will that help me?"

"If you mean to get a job, no. But you couldn't hope that it would, surely? It would have nothing to do with your qualifications. Besides, there aren't any jobs here, and there won't be for several years. You know that."

"I guess I do, Jack. It's just the thing that's most on mind these days, and it pops out every chance it gets. But I won't get my hopes up."

"No; there's no point."

Give the guy credit, he's honest, and he did look unhappy. I said, "Jack, I've been down the list, and there are two or three possibles. My first instinct is that this is not a woman, that the dandyism you can smell in both letters is very much a male thing. Would you agree?" In saying this I was accepting his assumption that the writer really was an English instructor, without agreeing with it. At least it would keep me looking useful to Jack, give me a brownie point. You never know your luck.

"Could you find out?" He was hardly listening.

"I doubt it." And then I offered him a bone. "One thing is puzzling. Where are the other letters? The usual ones, one signed by six members of the Business faculty and the other signed by four English professors? Why is this just a two-voice debate?"

"Never mind the interestin' fuckin' puzzles, Joe. You can do your Agatha Christie thing later. Right now I just want to have a quiet word with this bloke, myself, and kick his arse up through his hat."

"Is it that serious? It will blow over, surely."

"That's what I say. But the president called me first thing this morning. Did you know the new option in Business — The History of Salesmanship — was his idea?"

"Oh, shit, no."

"Oh, dear, yes. So he wants to know who is pissing in his shoes."

"That the president's phrase or yours?"

"Look, Joe. This is serious, for me and for this department. Put your damn thinking cap on. Find this bugger."

I said, "Here's a thought, Jack. Maybe it isn't someone in our department.

He cut me off. "Of course it is. Find the bastard, Joe. Find him. Quick."

So I was to set aside all doubts; to act under orders. I didn't mind. At least it would keep my mind off Carole.

THERE WAS STILL NO WORD from Simmonds; now I had a missing instructor and some anonymous letters on my plate.

And a pregnant partner.

I also had a class to teach on Steinbeck's story, "The Chrysanthemums," a story I like teaching because it shows Steinbeck at his most interesting and his most corny. But I had hardly begun the class, just counted heads, as it were, when Ron Crabbe put up his hand.

In one way, this Ron Crabbe was more of a problem than the Slapshot Boys. In his case the problem was that he was too bright; he was a mature student (in his late twenties) who had dropped out of the education system seven or ten years before and now decided to come back. Because he didn't have the right qualifications from high school, he was obliged to take some introductory courses to show his ability and aptitude for a university education, but though he had been doing other things for about a decade he had also educated himself and he found most of the first-year courses, including mine, child's play. Most teachers in a post-secondary institute sooner or later come up against a student who might be brighter than they:

such students were rare at Hambleton, but Ron Crabbe was mine.

A sense of academic duty should have prompted me to try to engage with him beyond and outside the class, to make myself available to respond to his wider intellectual needs, but I didn't, for a couple of reasons. First, I'm not very good at that kind of mentoring. I don't know how the tutors at Oxford conduct themselves but whenever, in the very early days, I tried to take a student aside, to bring one out, intellectually, it didn't really work. Sometimes, in fact, I was made to feel that what the student thought outside the topic we were supposed to be discussing — "The Function of the Fool in Lear," perhaps — were none of my business.

The other reason, really an expansion of the same point but focusing on Ron Crabbe, is that he hardly ever made comments in class that I could use to start a dialogue, just sat there with an ever-ready smile, a smile containing no hint of smugness, or contempt, or even superiority — a smile of a surprising sweetness on the face of a twenty-eight-year-old late bloomer; a smile left over from the days of the flower children. The other students liked having him around; they even seemed rather proud of him.

Thus I was wary of Crabbe, because from the start his obvious intelligence coupled with the absence of the intellectual's usual weapon (and armour) for dealing with the world — wit — made him hard to know. So far we had got along well because he liked me. It was that simple. I don't think there was much respect for my learning — you don't get to display a lot of that in first year, even if you have any — or admiration for my lecturing skills. Everything I said was obvious to him but he let me pontificate in peace to his less-educated fellow students. I was grateful for that, but I would still rather he went away.

Now his hand shot up as soon as the class was quiet, but his question was not about Steinbeck. He wanted to know if I was following the debate on Business Education in *The Rag*.

I was surprised. He rarely asked a question that wasn't on a point of information, like, "What exactly is a petard, sir?" so I took the opportunity, even though it was a digression, to respond by asking him what he thought of the debate in *The Rag*.

He said it seemed to him to be a classical debate, in that the writers' positions were grounded in emotion rather than reason, like people's political convictions, so while it was interesting, neither side was persuasive.

The class looked at him in wonder, and then at me, but I stepped back. "I wish I'd said that," I said, and added, "I didn't actually think much about it because the letters were anonymous. Always ignore anonymous letters, I say. They denote cowardice and spite. Now let's get on."

His hand had come up again, and then he dropped it and smiled, apparently accepting my response, for the moment, anyway.

THE HIGHLIGHT OF THE DAY came in the evening, as it so often did lately, as once more Carole had spent the day tying her own *bouquets garnis*. The change in her from the woman who had regarded working in the kitchen as one of the drawbacks of a heterosexual relationship to Julia herself still awaited comment: she didn't want to talk about it, cutting off my curiosity with responses like, "You like it? Enjoy." (Rather as I imagine her great-grandmother might have responded to an enquiry about a newly discovered interest in sex.) The results for me were wonderful but as I wondered I also feared to analyze the causes too closely in case she reverted to her old self. There was something of a fairy tale about what was happening; built into it was the caution that if I said the wrong thing, or anything at all too much, someone would wave the wand and I would be back eating beans on toast, so I shut up.

Tonight was fish. I'm not crazy about fish; we didn't have much of it when I was a kid, nor did the people we knew in Winnipeg, so I came to Toronto knowing only about fish fingers and oblong pieces of salmon. Over the last three months, Carole had ranged, in a culinary way, over the wide spectrum of the fish available in the St. Lawrence Market, including sea bass, sardines (the big ones), and smoked haddock, which she made into a pie. I went along with it, assuming that her body was telling her what she needed, only drawing the line at anything that still had its head attached when it came on the plate, and eels.

Tonight she served gravlax followed by clam chowder. A simple meal, she called it, but it was enough to make me want to move to Norway, or even the east coast, somewhere where this stuff was on offer all the time.

CHAPTER EIGHT

THE NEXT DAY, EIGHTEEN MEMBERS of the English department were tracking in and out of their offices, eyeing each other's backs as they passed in the corridor, trying to guess who among them was the "English Instructor" writing letters to *The Rag*.

Betsy Blue dropped into my office to see if I had any ideas. Betsy left South Africa wanting to be an actress but she only got as far as the maids' parts in touring companies, and she realized that her brains offered her more security than her acting talent. She came to us via an M.A. in drama at the University of Toronto. She came before I did, one of the people who got in under the wire without a Ph.D., but as well as her M.A. she has a first class B.A. from Leeds and doesn't take any shit from colleagues who claim the right to teach courses because they have a Ph.D. from Iowa. There was a famous moment when someone who had done his thesis on the critical history of *Frankenstein* — that is, the history of the criticism of *Frankenstein* — claimed the right to teach our course on the Gothic novel. Betsy Blue, who taught the course, asked, in committee, how he would approach the following novels and reeled off a dozen no one had heard of. Betsy then proposed that the course be taught by a generalist rather than risk having it distorted by an undue emphasis on someone's hobby horse, and thus restricted to a single work. It was unfair, of course; Betsy was prepared and the other one wasn't.

"What about Martin Love?" she asked now. "No, he's not bright enough. Those are good letters. Giles, then. No, he couldn't resist telling us, could he? Timothy? He's got a nice wit. What do you think, Joe?"

She was enjoying herself, but I didn't feel like joining in the fun. I actually didn't have any thoughts, and when I did, I would share them only with Jack. An English department is no place to start rumours. I said, "Betsy, you're the only one I can think of who has the wit to write those letters. 'A-ha,' I thought, 'the Spinster from South Africa. This is her hand!' How about you? Did you think maybe it was me?"

I was trying not to get trapped into a genuine speculation, even with Betsy. I already had the feeling that the issue might get very big and I didn't want Betsy or anyone else quoting me.

Betsy stood up. "I was going to suggest coffee, but you're obviously not in the mood for a chat. And I was married once. Twice actually, though never for long."

THERE WAS NO MESSAGE FROM Simmonds the next day, nothing to explain his absence and reassure me it was temporary. I felt very uneasy. I wondered if I had a real problem, not of an instructor who cancels his classes at the first hint of a cold, but of some kind of breakdown. In the ten years I've been at Hambleton, there have been at least three cases in the arts division of instructors who have concealed their problems long enough to be hired, but revealed them immediately once they started teaching. Two of them simply went back home to Alberta and Newfoundland, respectively, and one had to be committed. We've had no problems like that for a long time because the people who do the hiring now take their time over the process so that candidates who need treatment usually break down in the second or third interview. But in the extension division, we operate under a time constraint. We count the number of students who have paid fees, then hire instructors.

I found a telephone number for Simmonds in the course file that Myfanwy keeps. It was the number of a Jubilee Hotel — not a hotel I'd ever heard of. When I called, they told me they had never registered anyone called Simmonds, not this year, anyway. They offered to take a message in case such a person appeared, but I didn't bother. Leaving behind a false address sounded like the behaviour of a man with a plan.

But something might have happened to him. I called my boss at the detective agency to tell him my problem, asking him how I could find out if Simmonds was in jail or the morgue, or just in hospital. My boss is a former Metro policeman, and he still maintains the kinds of contacts that are useful. He said he'd find out for me, and call me back. "He's let you down, eh?" he added. He sounded angry, which should have surprised me, because I thought maybe Simmonds really was sick or even dead, the victim of an accident, perhaps; but I took it that my boss was feeling sympathy with me, caught in an awkward situation.

THE PRIVATE FILES OF THE full-time faculty are kept locked up in the Personnel department, and in theory are only available to department heads and above. The files of the temporary faculty, though, the sessionals, the part-timers and the other hourly workers stay within the department and even the pettiest of academic officials can have a look. I turned to Simmonds' personal file, knowing it wouldn't be very illuminating.

Some of these files can be very thick, because many of the temporary staff applied for a full-time appointment, then took whatever was available, temporarily. Thus there is sometimes a curriculum vitae, several letters of support from the candidate's pals, a description of a thesis, even an abstract and the first chapter. More usually, though, the sub-files of the extension department faculty are pretty slim. All we really need to know is that the candidate is qualified, preferably by having taught the course or something similar before, and that he is not wanted by the police. We like a couple of names we can call by way of references, but the interview is the chief tool for deciding suitability. As a senior clerk in the extension department advised me, "Try to get close to them in the interview. If they don't actually smell of drink, they're probably okay, and don't forget, these guys don't have a contract, in fact they've got no legal rights whatever, so they don't usually look for trouble."

Simmonds had come along at the last minute. He wanted to try teaching, wanted, I remembered, to get out of office work into another career. He had a degree in Communication Arts from Shrewsbury College, a technical institute in Northville, Michigan, and lots of practical experience.

I remembered that he had first applied by phone and I had asked him to come in right away because I needed someone more or less immediately. His written application was a single sheet of paper. There was a photograph attached, something we had recently requested in order to issue security passes to the faculty and staff. I unclipped it and slipped it into my pocket. The only notation on the sheet was the name of the registrar, Herb Mullins, in my handwriting.

I went into a trance to recover the memory of Herb's relevance. Simmonds had used his name as a reference, someone I could ask about him. I had put a tick against it, which indicated that I had checked with Herb. Deeper into my trance I found a conversation in which

Herb had told me that he had met a man at a party who was trying to help the son of a friend get into teaching, and he had referred him to me.

I called Herb now, to see if he could remember anything about Simmonds. He suggested that I should come by for coffee.

In his office, I repeated the question

He said, "Should I remember him? Or should it be, 'Ought I to ...'?"

"Never mind that, now. You recommended him."

"Yeah? How's he doing, then?"

"He's gone missing. He didn't turn up for his last class, and I've heard nothing from him since. He's disappeared. Where did you get him?"

"I'm trying to remember. Somebody asked me if I knew of any teaching positions, and I told him to ask you."

"Someone you met at a party, was it?"

"Might have been. If it was me, I was probably shit-faced." Herb was keeping his distance, looking the questions over before he responded, being careful. I should have wondered why.

"What was your impression of him?"

"Me? I never saw the guy. But I must have trusted the one who recommended him, whoever that was. Who else have you asked?"

"My boss at the agency. He's checking around the hospitals and the morgue. And the cops, of course."

"The cops?" He sounded alarmed. "Why the cops?"

"In case he's been arrested for something."

Herb subsided a little. "Oh. Yeah. Sure. And?"

"Nothing. Any other ideas?"

He shook his head. "Maybe you shouldn't worry about him."

"He's got a class next week. I need to know if he'll be there."

"What if he isn't? You could do it yourself, couldn't you? It's not that difficult."

Where had I heard that before? "I haven't got the time. Besides, I'm already being paid two hours for administering the program; they wouldn't pay me double. And I'm not doing it for free. I've done one class, and will probably have to do another. That's enough."

"Fucking right." He slid himself closer to his desk and started to move some papers around as if he was about to demonstrate a three-card trick. "I've got another idea. Wanda could do it. She was telling me she taught a little course on letter-writing over at Humber."

"Yes? I hope we won't need her, but I'll keep her in mind."

Herb was trying to be helpful but something was embarrassing him. He's not very good at being duplicitous. Our relationship is a pleasant tangle of just liking each other and respecting each other; now he seemed uneasy, wary. I guessed that he was feeling unhappy about being associated in Simmonds' hiring in case Simmonds turned out to be a problem.

AFTER LUNCH I GOT A call from Atkinson at the agency. Simmonds' name hadn't appeared on any police or hospital records in the last two days. He said, "You should line up someone else in case the guy's disappeared for good."

I said, "Everyone wants to write him off, but I'd like to find the body."

So where was he now? As with the regular faculty, there is always a slight possibility that a new teacher in the extension division will take fright before his first class. But the man I interviewed was not a man to panic. He might walk out, but he'd never run.

I let myself into the office Simmonds shared with all the rest of the night school teachers — those who taught only at night and had no other office. The Bull Pen, we called it. It was no more than a waiting room, a place to sit if they arrived too early for a class. Our night teachers carry their work with them, and I did not expect to learn anything useful, but I was surprised. There in the middle of one of the desks was a file, an inch thick, with Simmonds' name and the title "Correspondence for Business" on the cover. Inside was a page listing the twelve topics, one for each week of the session. I found something familiar about the topics but put that down to the fact that there can't be a lot of room for creativity in such a subject.

The file showed that six lessons had been prepared and, one by one, six delivered. The top lecture in the pile now was Lesson Seven, "The Letter of Complaint." A neatly typed outline was clipped to eight pages that had been photocopied from a text. I looked at a couple of the other lessons: each one was a chapter, drawn from the same text, behind a covering outline.

There was nothing wrong with this, especially in the case of this subject. He was simply doing what we all do when stuck at the last minute with teaching a course we know nothing about. Each week you put together a lecture and then deliver it, keeping just ahead of the class.

Simmonds had made up a class list, with the names of those attending each night ticked off. We aren't usually so methodical with non-credit courses, partly because a quarter of the intake has usually disappeared by the third week, and if you still have half of them at the end of the term you can count yourself singularly gifted. Simmonds' attendance records showed that he had handled the class and himself well. Three-quarters of them were still coming, a very respectable record.

CHAPTER NINE

THE DESK CLERK AT THE Jubilee Hotel was a good-looking fellow, thirty-ish, with a shaven head and a still demeanour. I reminded him of my call, and asked him if he was sure they had never registered Simmonds. He was sure. Then, because I had had an idea, I described Simmonds in as much detail as I could, and added that I thought he might have stayed six or seven weeks.

He shook his head.

Now I showed him the picture I had taken from Simmonds' file. The clerk raised his eyebrows. "You're talking about Johnny Tosti," he said. "He left two days ago. You're the second person enquiring after him. Someone came this morning, a pal of his, he said."

"How long was he here for? Tosti, I mean."

"May I ask who is calling?" he said in a parody of a secretary.

"I'm his boss. He didn't turn up for work. I'm worried about him."

The door to the street opened and the clerk's eyes slid sideways to see who it was. He had obviously worked out a stance, a way of presenting himself to the world. His mode was to stand absolutely still until a movement from hand or eye was called for, and then to move the part as economically as possible to accomplish its mission without help from the rest of his body. You used to be able to buy toys that did the same thing.

Now he consulted a file. "Three weeks. Practically a resident."

"The caller this morning," I said. "What did he look like?"

"You're his employer, right? Not a member of the Royal Canadian Mounted Police posing as his employer?" He accented the first syllable of "Police" comically.

"I'm his boss. Here's my security card from the college."

"In that case I would say the man who came looking for Johnny Tosti this morning was a plainclothes cop."

"You sure?"

"I've seen a few in my time. We all have around here."

"We?"

"Me and my friends. The cog-nos-cent-i. Is that how it's pronounced? Is it like 'poignant'?"

"How did he approach you this morning?"

"Head on. He didn't sidle." He leavened his delivery with a touch of camp, then returned to robot-ing.

"And he just asked for Tosti?"

"Johnny, he called him. 'Is Johnny still here?' he asked. Then he added the 'Tosti' in case I wasn't so pally with all the guests. 'No one of that name here,' I said, just in case Johnny Tosti was on the run, and he left. He seemed worried, you know, whipped out his cellphone and started talking cryptically to Al or Dave or somebody, the way they do."

"Has there been any message from Tosti since?"

"Not a word."

"And this is all you know about him?"

"How long is this going to go on? Sir, I never actually spoke to Tosti, ever. I knew who he was, that's all. In a week's time I might not recognize him if he comes through that door. I have an impression of a big clumsy guy. Now if you rotate yourself clockwise through two hundred and seventy degrees — "he flashed his eyes in the direction I would be facing if I rotated — "you will come face to face with one of our long-term residents. If anyone can help you, he can. He sits there all day watching the street, like an old tart whose feet hurt."

I rotated slowly as if I was sizing up the lounge and saw the subject of our conversation, a white-haired old man wearing a dirty grey cardigan with leather patches on the elbows. He smiled and nodded two or three times like Wemmick's father, guessing, I suspected, from the desk clerk's eyes that he was being talked about.

I walked over and sat down in the bamboo armchair opposite him.

"Looking for someone?" he asked.

I said I had arranged to meet a friend here, guy named Tosti. Did he know him?

"I know who you mean. A teacher of some sort, right?"

"Do you know anything about him?"

"I know where he lived. Here. Let's see what else I know. Oh yes, he was straight."

My mind had been wandering along some exotic paths since I had begun seriously wondering what might have happened to Simmonds, and I had already wondered if he had had to leave town quickly, or disappear underground for a while. That is, I had considered the possibility that he was some kind of villain, using Hambleton as a place to hide in, a possibility that had become more likely on hearing that a cop was looking for him. I was glad to hear that he was not a crook. "So he isn't in trouble with the law," I said.

"He might be," the old man said, a bit testily. "I just said he was straight. Lots aren't around here."

Now I heard what he was saying. I asked him how he knew, because mentioning the word would introduce the possibility that Simmonds was part of this world, perhaps Mr. Rough Trade himself who had been killed by one of his clients. What did I know?

"A little bird told me," he said, mocking the words as he said them,

Ah, well then. Yes. Nothing more to learn here.

As I passed the desk on my way to the street, the clerk said, to the space in front of him, "One more thing?"

I hesitated, my hand on the door.

"I have to report one more thing," he repeated.

"Report? Not to me. I'm not the authorities."

"Your friend Mr. Tosti may have gotten into bad company.

"Yes?"

"Yes. He carried a gun."

"You noticed one on him?"

"The maid did. When she came to clean his room the morning he left. He didn't answer when she knocked, so she thought he was gone already. When she stripped the bed she found a gun under the pillow. Just then your friend returned from wherever he had been — the bathroom, presumably, which, in the case of the cheaper rooms, is down the hall. Our Minda got out of there very quickly and a few minutes later, Tosti checked out. Then Minda told the housekeeper about the gun, and the housekeeper told me."

"And you told the police?"

"I considered it. I think now I should have called them and said, 'We have a tenant who had a gun under his pillow. He's gone now.' It just sounded a bit silly. But just in case, I'm telling you and if, as his employer, you consider it a matter for the gendarmerie, here's the phone."

"To get it off your mind?"

"It's off my mind already, now it's on yours. Odd, though, isn't it?"

"Can I talk to the maid?"

"You won't frighten her, will you?" He dialled a number on the house phone. "Paula," he said, "Is your Minda still around? Ask her to come to the desk, would you? Nothing wrong, no. No, nothing wrong with Minda or I'd be asking you to come to the desk, wouldn't I? I'm not her boss." He turned from the wall to face in my direction. "Two minutes," he said.

I said, "You had this job long?"

"Three months."

"You like it?"

"You meet all sorts," he said.

"I'll bet. Especially around here."

"I want to meet all sorts. I'm a writer."

As a wannabe myself, I wondered how far he had got along the road to publication. Was he having anything properly typed or printed out yet? I was saved from asking by the appearance of Minda, a woman in early middle age who looked as if she had the world by the tail, waving to the old man in the lobby and asking the clerk to guess what she had in her closed hand (a candy). Ready to leave for the day: a leather coat, Nikes, and a big grin. "I go home," she said. "My husband want me. There." She pointed out the window. Outside a dark blue BMW was waiting.

The clerk said, "This man wants to ask you about Mr. Tosti."

"He was a nice man," she said, her voice loud and clacky, but friendly. "A nice man," she repeated.

"But he had a gun," I said.

"Yes. I tell my husband. Kinky man I got. Sleeps with a gun, not a lady." She cackled.

"What kind?" I was curious to know if it was a pistol or a rifle. I didn't expect her to reply, *WalterPK.PO5* or some such.

"For the pocket." She slipped her hand under her T-shirt to show where she would keep it if she had a gun.

I slid the clerk's scratch pad towards me and drew a shaky outline of a revolver.

"No," she said. "Like this." She grabbed the pencil and made an equally bad drawing of the kind of automatic pistol S.S. officers in movies use.

The clerk took the pencil and tidied up the drawing, adding a wisp of smoke from the muzzle. This was for Minda's benefit.

"You draw good!" she cried. She showed me the drawing. "See? Good." She swung around and patted the now slightly fatuous-looking desk clerk on the cheek. "See you tomorrow, Roberto." She ran through the door to the waiting car.

"She seems very cheerful," I said, filling a bit of the void she had left behind.

"It's her way," he said. "She's got three jobs, a family to cook for, and I've never seen her look tired. I once thought of asking her to write out her diet to see what fuels her, but it'll turn out to be cod, bean stew, and that chicken they eat."

"What does her husband do?"

"He's a construction worker. He fell off the scaffolding and he's been on compensation for the last two years. Now he's her chauffeur, driving her from job to job."

I put the drawing in my pocket. "She's got a nice car, Roberto," I said.

He said, "All Portuguese cleaning ladies have nice cars. And my name is Robert."

AT HOME, CAROLE SAID SHE had been too busy to cook anything special. Did I mind chicken cacciatore?

CHAPTER TEN

SIMMONDS' DEFECTION HAD COME AT the wrong time for me. Teaching Business Correspondence is a long way from teaching Coleridge, but it is still teaching. The prospect of not being allowed to teach anymore — me, I mean — was making me angry, and the anger was landing on Simmonds. I wanted badly to find him, to tell him what I thought of him, never mind the compelling excuse he would have for why he went away.

I took my leave of the desk clerk and headed out along the Danforth to see if my boss at the detective agency had any other advice or suggestions.

Atkinson said, "You're not going to find him. He doesn't want to be found, it looks like. You should forget it and catch up on your marking. I mean, a guy sits in a cheap hotel room on Jarvis, teaching letter-writing at night, carries a gun, disappears. What are the possibilities?"

"He's dead?"

"That's the big one. So you'll have to wait for him to surface in the lake."

"But what was he doing?"

"Maybe the job he came to do is done."

"You mean like he's a hit man? Teaching Business Correspondence? And he's got the wrong kind of name, surely. David Simmonds?'

"Johnny Tosti?"

"But that's his alias."

"Which? But I agree with you. A hit man teaching Business Correspondence would be a first."

"What are the other possibilities? "

"If he's still alive?"

"Yes."

"Maybe he's just pretending."

"To do what?"

"To be a night school teacher."

"Or to be a gunman of some kind?"

"Right. Maybe he was just picking up atmosphere. Maybe he wants to be a novelist."

Atkinson was just teasing me. He knew about my own ambitions. His kind of wit might have been good to have on a long stakeout, but it got on my nerves sometimes.

"Look, what's the procedure if someone goes missing? What do the cops do?"

"They're like everybody else these days. They put it on the computer. Then, when they can spare a man they send him around to the missing guy's home and his workplace to ask questions. Anyone seen him lately? Did he have a girlfriend? Where's she? That kind of thing. Then, unless he's some kind of suspect, they wait."

"How long?"

"Until he turns up."

"And if he doesn't, say, after a year?"

"His relatives might hire someone like us to look for him.

Otherwise, they just wait until the law declares him dead, then they share out his money."

I GOT TO THE OFFICE early the next morning because my Creative Writing class came in the middle of a heavy day, and my preparation was in a slightly underdone condition. Last week the class had been intrigued to discuss the difference between reminiscence, a sketch, and a real story — that is, a piece of fiction. At the end of the class I had put the question, "When is a story not a story?" and now I needed to lead the discussion to respond to the question.

I was full of the beginnings of ideas last week but none of them had jelled properly, because I hadn't done enough work, and now I couldn't remember them. I did have an old trick up my sleeve but if I used that, I would have nothing in reserve for the rest of the term.

I sat at the desk trying to think my way into the problem but before I could even focus on anything, someone stood in the doorway.

"Yes?" I asked, meaning, fuck off.

"Joseph Barley?"

I winced. There is something about my fully articulated first name that makes me feel like an impostor, something to do with the totally opposed vibes of "Joseph" and "Joe." Vladimir Petrov uses the full "Joseph," but with a soft "J," which makes me sound like a character in a German film. I nodded and waited.

"Constable Sargent," he said and waited for the name to register. Then, "Metro Police."

I said, "You get a lot of jokes about your name?"

He smiled and came in, picking up a chair from the back wall and twirling it in place in front of my desk. "Nothing to what I'll get when

I'm promoted," he smiled again. He had a large pink-and-white, permanently smiling face, and wavy yellow hair. He didn't seem like a cop, more like a greeter at a casino.

"I was thinking of the painters. Constable and Sargent." I said.

"About them, too. That's how I spell it. My granny thought we were related. She looked a bit like *Whistler's Mother*, herself. You know about ...?"

"I know about *Whistler's Mother*."

I watched him sit, projecting hard my irritation at having been interrupted, keeping my pencil in the air. State your business, buddy, my body language said.

He looked around. "Nice office."

This was patently sucking up. The virtue of my office is that it is mine, that I don't share it with anybody. It is a grungy little room without even a window, painted goat-vomit green. David Simmonds had been unimpressed.

Sargent sat there, smiling in friendly fashion as if it was his office, and I had come to see him. I said, "Can I help you, Constable?"

"I doubt it," he said. "I was always pretty good at English, except for poetry."

I thought, I can outwait you. Whatever you're up to, you're going to have to say it.

Finally, he said, "I'm really looking for a guy named Simmonds, David Simmonds."

"Aren't we all?" I said. "I reported him missing to you people yesterday."

"Right. Right. That's why I'm here. He hasn't come back, then?"

"No."

"Have you done anything about it?"

"I reported it, to you guys, yesterday."

He nodded, and stopped smiling. I was finally getting under his skin.

But he had his way of getting back. "You're a private investigator, right, Joseph?"

I said, "My friends call me Joe; people I've just met call me 'Mister,' especially if they're younger than me." Rude, but I was still trying to think about my Creative Writing class while he was tick-tocking my preparation time away.

"Right," he said. "Different generations, eh? Point is, I'm looking for David Simmonds, and I find his boss is, too, and his boss is a private eye. That what you call yourself?" He snickered. "So I have to wonder if you've done a little sleuthing of your own, and found anything that might be helpful to us. No?"

"I've tried to find him, yes."

"As I say, any luck?"

"He checked out of the place he was staying three days ago and hasn't been seen since. How did you know I work for a detective agency?"

"Big Brother. The computer. It's standard now. Get a name, run it up, see if there's a record."

"You did that with my name?"

"Yup, and there you were on our list. So I came down to see if you had any ideas that might save us some work. We're very understaffed."

"Is this normal? Yesterday someone told me you guys don't get excited until there's some good reason to be."

"Guy goes missing in the middle of the — what ... Term? Semester? That sounds like a reason."

"Maybe he's got amnesia."

"Yeah, but why?"

"Or maybe it's just nerves. This was his first job. I'm worried that he's cracked up and is wandering the streets somewhere."

"That right? Or on a plane to Tibet, maybe?" He grinned, conspiratorially, one bullshitter to another. Then he switched it off, or down a little. "Look, don't get in too deep yourself, okay? You hear anything, let us know. Don't go down the hole on your own. Here's my card, though I don't really need a card with a name like mine. But anything at all, call me."

I said, "One thing. He's using an alias. He registered in his hotel as Johnny Tosti."

He looked at me as if he was thinking. "That's interesting. Yeah, that's the kind of thing." He put out his hand, I shook it, and he walked to the door. There, pausing, he said, "Tosti, right. You know him as Simmonds, though, right?"

I said, "That's his real name."

"Yeah, right," he said and left.

I STILL HAD A LITTLE time to whip up something for Creative Writing, but the appearance of Sargent had filled my head with questions. First, what was he doing here? His response to that was clever, but weak. The report that someone of no importance is missing doesn't generate much interest in police headquarters. I knew that. People leave their wives and husbands a lot these days, some of them without even a note. I've been on a few such cases myself. The appearance on the scene of Constable Sargent created the possibility that the logging of Simmonds' name in their computer had brought forth a question. Did Simmonds have a record, maybe? Then an obvious idea hit me and I phoned the Jubilee Hotel.

The desk clerk said, "Yes, I had second thoughts about not speaking to the police. After you left, one of their heavies appeared."

"Constable Sargent? Wavy hair? Big smile?"

"That's the one. He came looking for Johnny Tosti."

"And that's what he called him, Johnny Tosti?"

"No, but it didn't take long to figure out that's who he was looking for. Can I go back to work now?"

"I guess so." I hung up

So Sargent hadn't quite laid all his cards on the table with me. But then, he didn't have to. He showed enough of his hand, though, to signify that Simmonds/Tosti was an interesting guy, to the cops, anyway.

Using an alias is obviously duplicitous in intent, and I had another look at the meagre information that Simmonds had supplied on his background. I tried to call Shrewsbury College in Northville, Michigan, where Simmonds had earned his undergraduate degree. The operator in Detroit couldn't find such a college. I put in a call to Mike, an old graduate school friend living in Detroit who is now a senior executive in a company that manufactures wiper blades for the automobile industry. He put one of his secretaries on to it and she called back an hour later to say that, true, there was no such college in Northville, or, indeed, in the state of Michigan, and there never was one in the past, either.

Next and last I called the three business schools in Toronto, at one of which Simmonds had claimed to be pursuing an M.B.A. I had to go at it in a roundabout way, asking a man on the faculty of one of the colleges, a man who belongs to my tennis club and who is constantly asking me to play him (he isn't very good and he's quarrelsome on the court) to confirm that Simmonds wasn't a student at his college. He said such information was privileged.

I said, "Ah, come on now, Ted, this is negative information. It can't be used about someone, can it?"

He said, "Sometimes it is just as useful to a gambler to know that a horse won't win as it is to know that he will."

I said, "I told you that, last summer."

He said, "And you got it from Dick Francis."

Ted never forgets anything and always lets you know it. That's what makes him a good economist, I guess. He said, "But I suppose that when the enquirer is from another college, then he's privileged. All right."

I said, "Sometimes he uses an alias, calls himself Johnny Tosti. Could you make that part of your enquiry?"

There was a pause. "I don't like the sound of this? Are you calling as a private investigator?"

"No, no. As a college administrator, looking for a straying student. It's to do with a dud cheque. I'll explain on the court, the next time we play."

Ted liked the sound of that. He made the calls to the other graduate schools and learned that no such student was registered at either school, and called me right back to tell me. I'd nearly managed to hang up before he said, "Sunday? Can we play on Sunday morning?"

"Sure thing, Ted. Eight o'clock?"

It would be a tedious game and I'd be letting down my long-standing partner, but I thought I might as well get it over with.

"See you on the court," he said.

I put the phone down and went back to thinking about Carole, and babies, and jobs — or rather, trying not to think of these things, for in dealing with the world of lost instructors and letters in *The Rag* I was using only about one tenth of my mind. The rest was taken up with the real world.

CHAPTER ELEVEN

IT WAS TIME TO SUM up. So far I knew only that Simmonds had changed his name, and had moved without leaving a forwarding address. Not a lot to speculate with. Obviously he was either hiding out from someone looking for him, or he was trying to get close to someone without being noticed himself. Elementary.

The appearance of Constable Sargent seemed to say that the Toronto police were the people looking for him, that he was on the run from them. But Simmonds must have felt his cover was good enough if he planned to work for me for twelve weeks, and he wasn't worried that he would be recognized on the street.

Atkinson, the boss at my agency, was my source for anything I wanted to know from the police that was public knowledge — missing persons, crooks who had been let out of jail lately — that sort of thing. But because he had once been on the force and was now in business for himself, he was barred by the rules from knowing anything even slightly classifiable. That was how Atkinson explained it to me once.

I decided to try Sergeant Lewicki, an old student of mine who was now working in police headquarters on the staff of a deputy chief.

Lewicki was out, so I left a message with my name, and a query about Simmonds/Tosti. I didn't mention Sargent's visit, hoping that Lewicki and Sargent never crossed paths.

He called back half an hour later. "Sir," he said, in deference to our old relationship and before I could speak. "I'm not in the office right now, but I've just picked up my messages. About this guy, I can't help you. All I can say is, er, he's not one of us."

"You would know if he was?"

"Yes. Now, sir, please don't call me at the office for a while. There's an internal investigation going on; you must have read about it. Some guys on the squad are accused of being on the take and have been suspended, so calls from private detectives make us antsy."

"Is that why you're not calling from the office now?"

He hung up.

My head was aching and I reached for my Penguin book of Lawrence's stories, for relief and to keep Carole at bay and because I hadn't done that final glance at the text every class preparation needs. This time it took only a few minutes to look over the story. I've taught it a dozen times and hope to teach it a dozen more; but the whole thing is firmly in my head now and I was looking around for something else to fill the time when Herb Mullins came in, cursing. He closed the door behind him, pulled a chair close to the front of the desk, hit on it with both clenched fists, and said, "Tell me what to do, Joe. I've got the fucking Minister of Colleges and Universities arriving in twenty minutes for a little light supper in the boardroom, then, right after, we start the fall Convocation." He was distraught.

"You could order something in ..."

"Don't be an asshole!" he shouted. "Never mind the food. That's all laid on. My problem is how to hand out the degrees and diplomas."

"What's the problem? You've done it before, surely? I was there in the spring ..."

"Will you shut the fuck up? I haven't even told you the problem yet. You know how you give out the certificates?"

"I think so," I said, carefully. "But tell me again."

"They are on the table on the podium in two piles, one for the minister and one for Bluebell or whoever is standing in for him, like the dean. Each pile is in alphabetical order. The graduates come up in pairs and split as they approach the platform, one to Bluebell and the other to the minister. I've got good ushers who will have a list of the names in each pile so they can make sure the students go to the right guy. It's smooth as silk, or it has been. But here's the news: the minister's office has just called to ask us to make sure that his pile has all his constituents in it. Cocksucking politics."

"So what's the problem?"

"What's the problem? What's the fucking problem? I have an hour to feed this minister's face, kiss his ass, and set up the diplomas in the way he wants. You know what that means? I have to get a printout of all the students with their home addresses. Then I have to find out where the boundaries of this asshole's riding fall and match the riding with the addresses on the printout. Then I have to make up two new piles of certificates, and two new lists for the ushers. It can't be done."

But as he talked I was being visited by a solution like the Duke of Wellington's when Queen Victoria asked him what to do about the plague of sparrows in the new Crystal Palace. (He said, "Sparrow-hawks, Mum.") I now thought of an answer to Herb's problem so simple, so daring, that on a battlefield it would have immortalized me. I let him have it bit by bit, savouring it. I said, "How familiar is the minister with his constituents?"

Herb said, "How do you mean?"

I said, "Isn't he the one who was parachuted in? He lost out in his own riding in the last election, and the member for Coon County, or whatever it is, resigned so there would be a byelection which your man could run in and win. The other party put up a token candidate and their payoff was that their real man, the guy who should have run, and maybe won, was made a senator. Right?

"It sounds familiar. That's what they usually do."

"Then you don't have to worry. Let's go."

We trotted off to Herb's office while I explained. "All you have to do is label the two piles of certificates 'President' and 'Distinguished Guest,' and do the usual double check to make sure the first few names in each pile still correspond to the usher's lists. Let the minister know his pile has been carefully sorted. Have someone say 'They're all in order now' while he's listening. Maybe wink? No. Just say it very quietly."

You could see by his eyes that Herb's mind was racing to find the flaw. "And?" he said.

"Then just go ahead. Take the minister aside to tell him to be sure to stand by the pile earmarked for him, because though they are sorted, that's the kind of little thing that might go wrong, tell him. Then tell him that not everyone in his pile is from Coon County but that all the voters in Coon County are in his pile along with some others to keep the two piles even. Tell him it's like that philosophy thing, that syllogism, "All A is B but all B is not A ..."

"Fuck the syllogism thing. That'll just confuse this asshole. Why can't I just say, 'These are yours, dickhead'?" But he was starting to look looked pleased.

In all this it was nice to be again explaining something to Herb. For years, he's been helping me to compile a sort of "Child's Guide to WordPerfect," but lately I haven't had much in the way of grammar rules to offer him in exchange. I said, "Tell him just that there are a few oddballs in his bunch, so don't mention Coon County in case it gets into his head. You don't want him shaking hands with some

Chinese student from Hong Kong, telling her how proud Coon County is of her. He'll understand that. He's going to have to be satisfied that he'll be doing himself some good, somewhere in his pile. Smile at them all, tell him."

"Should I let the ushers in on it?"

I've never seen Herb speak so deferentially to anybody, let alone me. "Just tell them you've labelled the piles to satisfy a request from the ministry that the minister's godson will be in the right pile." Solutions poured out of me. "Don't tell them or anybody else — not a word. You don't want the story in *The Hambletonian*, let alone the other rag."

Herb giggled. "Christ, Joe, I believe you've done it. Now I have to run and meet this bastard. I owe you, Joe. A big one."

LATER, I WAS SERVED A dinner of pork chops Normandy (apples, cream, Calvados) followed by a new cheese Carole had discovered. Cheese in our house used to be orange or white, made from cows' milk, packaged in slabs at the factory in Stratford, Ontario in the last three months. Lately it has come from regions as formerly unknown to me as Asturias, or Galicia, and from almost any animal. This cheese was soft, with a hard, dark brown skin, making it look like the kind of change purse you open by pressing the sides. It was delicious.

It had occurred to me to wonder if there was a deeper reason for the new interest in cooking than merely a change of taste. Cooking had certainly not become a substitute for sex, which was holding up nicely, thank you. Now, as I watched her push herself with more and more difficulty between the table and the sideboard, I had another thought. "Do you think that your, er, new interest in cuisine is sort of a way of er, escaping thinking about this other thing?" I looked at what I was talking about.

"This?" she said, patting her belly. "Taking my mind off this? What a nutty idea! I like thinking about it. I don't need distraction."

CHAPTER TWELVE

HERB CALLED ME THE NEXT day to say that everything had gone smoothly, and to thank me. "So what's up with you?" he asked, being polite.

I started to tell him but he interrupted. "Pick up some coffee and join me," he said. "I told you, we owe you a big one."

"I SEE THEY'RE WRITING LETTERS again, the little gob-shites," he said in his office. Like most non-academic administrators he enjoyed watching the faculty squabble.

"One of them is, anyway."

"And you don't know who this piss-head is, right?"

"How would I know?"

"Why don't you do an analysis of his style, kind of a Professor Higgins-type thing only with script. Can that be done?"

I took this in, rejected it, then thought about it a bit. Was it possible? "Not by me," I said, answering my own question.

He winked. "Fake the fucker," he said. "Do an analysis. Get the psychos to help you. Find out that the letter displays the characteristics of a compulsive wanker with pederastic tendencies, or a latent kleptomaniac who might kill if he's cornered. Say you've asked the student newspaper to let you know exactly how they got the message, whether in a document you could send to the police lab, or by traceable email. Say you've ..."

"Herb."

"I haven't finished."

"Herb."

"Yeah?"

"Shut up. This could be nasty. Bluebell is very unhappy."

"Ah, right. Himself is involved." He stopped grinning. "Is that what you wanted to talk about?"

"I came to ask you if you had any more thoughts about Simmonds."

I brought him up to date on what I'd found out so far.

He shook his head. "I did phone the guy who asked me to put in a word for him, but it's been a couple of months now and he can't even remember what it was all about."

"Do you have his number?"

"Yes, but I think he left for Europe already. Got any other ideas?"

"Not so far."

"You could forget it. I know someone who could teach his class."

"Wanda, you told me."

"Her, too, but I was thinking now of Sylvia Tarka, the comptroller's wife. She's a C.A. and she does consulting work, teaching other C.A.'s how to write letters. She taught Business Correspondence at night in the Business department for years until one of the full-time people wanted her course to tidy up his own timetable. Now he teaches all day Monday and three hours Monday night, and that's his week's work. The rest of the time he's got an office downtown where he consults, for Chrissake."

In some moods, Herb was mildly contemptuous of most of the faculty, finding the notion of tenure just a boondoggle. Nobody in Oshawa had tenure. As we had recently learned, General Motors could pack their bags and go back to Michigan tomorrow and ten thousand people would be out of work. But Herb reserved his real contempt for those who complained about their workload while holding down other jobs off campus.

I said, "I remember him now. He wanted to double up his classes, too, didn't he, so he wouldn't have to come in too early on Monday mornings? He wanted to avoid the traffic from cottage country on Sunday night."

"That was someone else, guy who taught Crisis Management. Never mind him, hire Sylvia."

"You like her, don't you?"

"Yeah." Herb smiled. "That's okay, isn't it? Should you only hire people who give you a pain in the ass, so you know you're being fair?" This was Herb showing where his world stood on affirmative action.

"If Simmonds doesn't turn up next week, she can apply to start the week after."

"I'll tell her. He won't turn up."

"Why are you so sure he won't turn up?"

He looked confused for a moment. "It's the way he went," he said. "Like somebody whacked him."

Herb likes to show he's still in touch with the real world, the world where guys get whacked, like on *The Sopranos*.

I said, "I wish I could tell you how wrong you are, based on my acquaintance with the man, but I can't. I know nothing about him, I've realized. I don't even have an address for him anymore. But saying that gives me an idea: I do have his SIN number. Maybe the police could trace it."

"I thought the SIN was sacred — you know, secret. No one was supposed to know about it except you and the Auditor General."

"That was when it started. It's changed a lot."

"So try it. But don't forget Sylvia can do his job if you need her."

"How do you know? Have you been talking to her?"

Again he looked a little uncomfortable. "I had coffee with her the other day. She mentioned it. You know, just chewing the fat."

ATKINSON PROMISED TO FEED THE SIN number into his pipeline and tell me what came out. He said, "Don't get your hopes up. Might be three months before he surfaces, depending if he was dumped into one of the larger lakes."

I said, "Have you been talking to Herb Mullins?" It certainly sounded like it.

"Who?"

"You know who — the registrar here. He says Simmonds may be dead, too."

"Yeah? It's an obvious conclusion, I guess. I wouldn't waste any more time on it."

"It's my professional pride. Also, Herb has got someone lined up to do Simmonds' job, but I have to find Simmonds first to cross him off."

Before I left the office I made one more call, to my old china (that's his word) Professor Boris Fish, of York University. The question I put to him was who, among the linguists of his acquaintance, would be most likely to identify a fine American hand in a piece of English prose. Or any other kind of hand: a female hand, for instance, would that show up?

Boris said, "You want a handwriting person, not a linguistics specialist. Find yourself a gypsy."

I said, "I don't have a manuscript, just the text of some letters."

"Then you're asking a lot, mate. What's this all about?"

I told him about the letters in *The Rag*, and how I wondered if an expert could identify the writer by his syntax.

He said, "Fax the letters to me. I'll show them to Clapton. The best man would be de Angelis but he's away on a double sabbatical, won't be back for two years, so I'll try Cyril. Professor Clapton to you. He's the only one I can think of. I'll call you. I'm coming down your way tomorrow. Shall I drop in for a cup of tea on the way home?"

He meant around midnight and for a dozen beers, not a cup of tea, but I'm getting too old for that. I said. "Let me get this thing out of the way, first. It's getting me into night work. Besides, Carole goes to bed by ten, so if you came by at your usual time ..."

"I'd catch you doing the old Sir Roger de Coverley. No, surely. She must be nearly due. Sorry. Thinking out loud. Right you are. Let me know when you want to do some male bonding. Usually happens with pregnant husbands about now."

TIMOTHY COTTER PUT HIS HEAD around the door. "Lunch?" he asked.

Timothy joined the department last year from one of the colleges in the Maritimes, where, he said in his interview, he was fed up with being the token gay in the department, and cramped by the social life available in Scrod Harbour. Frankly, he said, he did not hanker after the research possibilities of Toronto; most of what he needed he could get on his laptop: what he wanted was culture and a social life. (He pronounced it *kulchah*, then and always, to lighten the word a bit, but he meant it. He is a good amateur violinist whose major hobby is playing chamber music.) He plucked all the liberal strings, and the committee liked him, too. He is a specialist in CanLit and a published poet, thus ringing all the correct literary bells, and when he told them he was gay, the gong went off. Having no other gays in the department, we were out of step with the times.

The other thing to remark on is his clothing. He is about my age, forty, and he is our man from the Ivy League — neat dark grey trousers of very thin flannel, brogues, a jacket of soft tweed, a button-down shirt and a repp tie.

He waited now for my response, smiling his sweet crewcut smile, like a member of the Harvard rowing eight.

I shook my head. At any other time I'd have been glad to join him but I wanted to do the class preparation that the Simmonds affair had interfered with.

"I see," he said. "Busy, busy, busy. Give Carole my love, then."

I WENT DOWN TO OUR cafeteria for some coffee and a chocolate bar to keep me going, and there in the lineup, as I was musing whether Carole's interest in *Talk to Her* was connected with the fact that the main figure in the movie is a woman in a coma who becomes pregnant, I was accosted by someone who looked familiar, a mature student.

"Arnold Straker," he said. "I'm in Mr. Simmonds' class." He shook my reluctant hand. He was a man of about twenty-five; his suit was neat and clean but rendered lifeless by dry cleaners, a man who had to live economically. Only his gloves pointed to the man he was aspiring to be, expensive yellow pigskins that he kept on the table in front of him, handling them occasionally as we talked.

I said, "I'm not staying. I just picked up some coffee to take back to my office."

"Spare me a minute," he said, not asking, treating me like a colleague, pointing to the table he had already staked out.

I followed him and sat down, but without opening the lid of my coffee cup.

When he saw I really meant not to stay, he said, "Will you be taking the class next week?"

Still no "sir" or "Mr. Barley," and someone like this would have remembered or found out my name. My instinct about him was sound. He was very clearly an "insider" type, one who liked to show he was in the know.

All English teachers are paranoid. Doing our own thing, we always have some room for the fear that students will not find our thing as interesting, challenging or generally as worth listening to as Professor Blood's thing which they got last year. Sometimes when, no matter how hard you flog yourself, it has become impossible once more to get students to respond to the side-splitting humour of Pope's "Essay on Man," or even keep half of them from closing their eyes, you yearn to be teaching something concrete like Geography with all those maps and charts and field trips, or History with its names and dates and causes and effects, and amusing little anecdotes about Abraham Lincoln's sex life, and the relationship of Mackenzie King and his dead dog. All this surges up when a student like Starkey asks a question like that.

"Why?" I said, lifting up my coffee, keen to be on my way.

"I just wondered."

"Why?" Might as well grab it by the horns. "Do you miss Mr. Simmonds?"

"He was a pretty good teacher, but I won't miss him, no."

Ah. "Why, then?"

"It's just that I don't know which class to prepare for, his on 'The Letter of Complaint,' or yours on the other seven uses of the comma."

"You've already got Mr. Simmonds' class ready, haven't you? And besides, you'll need them both eventually. It wouldn't be too hard to be ready for either, would it?"

"No, but the thing is, I saw Mr. Simmonds last night, so I thought he might be coming back." He tried to say it casually, but he knew it was a significant piece of news and he delivered it as a child would. ("There's a man lying down on the sidewalk outside and his hair's on fire.")

"You saw him? Where?" I no longer kept my distance. This was a lot better than pedagogical paranoia.

"In a coffee shop on Church Street."

"Whereabouts? Anywhere near Cumbrae's Meats?"

"You know it?"

"I know Cumbrae's Meats. It's the only place I do know on Church."

"This coffee shop is in the same block."

"Did you speak to him?'

"No. See, let me explain. I was in there to meet a couple of friends I've known since high school. One of them is an optometrist and the other's a barber — hairdresser, I guess. He charges forty bucks for a haircut."

"Is this relevant?"

"What?"

"What your pals do for a living. I'm kind of busy."

"I guess not. The thing is we've stayed in touch. I like coffee-housing with these guys, though I'm not gay myself."

"I see. But they are."

"That's what I mean. They have good jokes, those guys. Anyway, I saw this character way down the dark end of the room, shaved head, granny glasses, earring — you know?"

"Mr. Simmonds? Are you kidding?"

"Let me tell it. This guy caught my eye, or I caught his, and I thought he was about to try to pick me up, but he cut off the contact right away and went back to his reading. A little book, it was, probably one of those reissued classics. There was something about him, and I asked my buddies if they knew him. They didn't, and they are regulars there, it's where I meet them, so he wasn't. A regular, I mean. He left pretty soon after that, and we all got a good look. My buddies came up blank, but something stuck with me. Then walking along Wellesley to the subway, I got it. This guy was missing a tooth, here." He pointed to the tooth next to one of his incisors. "The same tooth that Mr. Simmonds was missing in the last class. Then I really concentrated to see if it was a coincidence, and I worked out that although he looked nothing like Mr. Simmonds now, all the differences between them were really superficial. You know? Hair and glasses, mostly, plus he'd shaved off that bloody great moustache. Then I saw the thing he couldn't cover up, that walk of his. You ever see him walking from behind? The way he sort of flicks his feet forward then lurches after them? As I was watching him, he nearly fell over a street-person, sitting by the curb, begging, just the way he used to be bumping into people at school. This guy was Simmonds in makeup, I'm sure of it."

"What do you think he was doing?"

"Getting his kicks — I mean metaphorical kicks. You know, like an accountant by day, a drag queen by night."

"But he wasn't in drag. If you're right, what was he dressing up as?"

"You'd have to know more about the culture. It changes all the time. Couple of years ago my buddies used to dress up in jeans and checked shirts and those big yellow boots, lumberjacks. Only at night."

"You putting me on?"

"Make allowance for the fact that I get most of this second-hand. They could have been teasing me about the lumberjack stuff, they're great for that and I never actually saw them dressed up — but I don't think so. Anyway, the bottom line is I have seen Simmonds at night in a gay area, looking like I've told you."

"I don't know what to say," I said. I really didn't.

"Do you think he'll come back to teach us?"

I didn't shrug immediately, but thought about it — Straker's question, not shrugging. "I've no idea," I said. "It depends what he's up to, I guess. Officially I've heard nothing. What do you think? Your guess is as good as mine."

"I'd say not. He'd have phoned in some story by now, wouldn't he?'

"So what's he up to?" I tried something on Straker. "You think he's been outed? You say you know the scene better than I do. Could someone have seen him in a gay bar?"

"That wouldn't mean anything. You're a bit out of date. A lot of people, men and women, go to gay bars for a night out, the way they go to tango clubs. Mainly in couples, sure, like tourists, but not always."

"Tango clubs?" Out-of-date was right; I was beginning to feel that Carole and I were the archetypal couple of country mice and it was all her fault. She doesn't dance.

"There are a couple of clubs on Adelaide where you go just to tango. One of them doesn't even have a liquor licence. People who go there are serious dancers. You can go alone, too."

"So Simmonds may be just dressing up and have been seen by someone like you and feels he can't face the class?"

"Doesn't that sound possible?"

"If it was Simmonds you saw, then he's only been doing this thing for a couple of weeks at most, unless he's into wigs, a shaved-head one when he's out at night or a hairpiece when he's teaching." I tried to recover a bit of the student/teacher relationship. "Frankly, I don't think it was Mr. Simmonds," I said.

He stood up. "It was Mr. Simmonds. See you in class. Still the comma, right? I think you make it kind of interesting, with good examples and all."

Patronizing bastard.

I had to accept that he was probably right about Simmonds, but I could make no sense of it. On the face of it, it still looked as if Simmonds had been suddenly outed, and he'd panicked. But the note he left me surely argued against his having fled.

The thing to do was not to speculate. When my superiors asked, I would say I didn't know, it was a mystery. But the longer things went with no news from Simmonds, the angrier I would get. I'm not a model citizen; I can lie and cheat and steal with the best of them when no one is looking. I can understand that president of a Bible college, caught shoplifting, who said, "I went into the store intending to buy some caviar because all my life I wanted to taste real caviar. But it was a hundred and fifty dollars an ounce and I was raised a devout Baptist, and when I thought of all those starving African children I couldn't possibly justify spending that kind of money on an ounce of fish eggs, so I stole it and sent twenty-five dollars to Africa."

But I am a model citizen as far as my teaching duties go. Analyze my motives and you will probably find a mixture of duty (it's what I'm paid for), responsibility (I can't stand the idea of twenty students tramping through two feet of snow to an eight a.m. class in January to find I'm still in bed), and showbiz (as they said of Margot Channing in *All About Eve*, "If she can walk or crawl or drag herself to the theatre, she plays"). I will croak asthmatically through a class on "Christabel" just to show them, Carole says, what I will endure for their sake. She is half right, but it's the other half I'm talking about. Set aside the ego (I think), and there is still something left, a sacred duty to deliver the best of yourself — and of Coleridge, of course; a dedication to the work and to those faces in front of you who came to the university after a summer of shovelling shit to raise the fees, and who registered in your course, which is optional. Because they think, some of them, that it will be an enlarging experience, and even in the most cynical times, it sometimes is, even if you (the instructor) don't know when it might happen. The image that comes to mind is the one in Coleridge's "Frost at Midnight," when "the frost performs its secret ministry," creating its patterns on the window "unhelped by any wind." If you've been talking in lively fashion it's easy to know that the students are appreciating you as they nod and grin at your cleverness and jokes, and very warming it is. But it is the "secret" ministry that you have to believe in, the connections that are being made that you are not aware of. Recently I received a postcard from a former student, mailed in Grasmere in the English Lake District. The student had just visited Wordsworth's cottage and walked across a bit of Scafell Pike. "You were right," the message said. It was signed with a name I didn't remember. I looked it up and sure enough I had taught him five years before, but I still couldn't remember him.

Right about what? It doesn't matter. I put his postcard in my course file so I would come across it some winter morning when nobody in the class I was currently teaching seemed to give a pinch of coonshit about Michael and his sheepfold.

CHAPTER THIRTEEN

I RETURNED TO MY OFFICE just in time to catch the cleaner looking at something on my desk. He didn't look guilty when I walked in; just picked up the thing he was looking at and waved it at me. The photograph of Simmonds. "Who's he?" he asked. "I see him watching." Our cleaner is Portuguese, too.

Christ, I thought. The Scarlet Pimpernel. "Where did you see him? When?"

"Across the street from the Engineering office. Watching the store, the copy shop. Two or three times, about a couple weeks ago."

"Waiting for someone?"

"No, standing across the street, like watching to see someone come out. I thought he might be a ... you know ... watching a woman through the window."

"Where did he go?"

"He walked back in to the building."

"How come you remember him?" And no bullshit about a missing tooth, please.

"I remember him the way you remember someone standing outside your house, watching. That's what he was like."

"Did he look like that?" I pointed to the picture.

"Sure. I'm telling you. That's who I saw."

It was no good trying to prepare classes after that. I made a couple of notes of things I could do in an emergency, finding an exercise I kept handy, a large paragraph of hard-to-punctuate prose that we could all correct together, after they had used up some of the time trying it on their own. Ron Crabbe would do it in five minutes but it would keep the others busy, and Crabbe always brought a book to the class to fill in the time.

Prepared, then, or at least, lightly armed, for the next day's encounters, instead of heading for the parking lot behind the building, I went out by the front door to speak to the security guards.

I took the picture of Simmonds with me. I wanted to find out if there had been any other unusual sightings of him lately. It was becoming clear that Simmonds was not what he seemed and I ran through the possibilities in my mind as they occurred to me. The first, obviously, was that he was leading some kind of double life, but one that might be harmless enough. If you're a timid bank clerk by day (why is it always a bank clerk who is timid? Why not a timid garbage collector or streetcar conductor?) it's not illegal at night to take charge of your dreams by dressing up as the Lone Ranger. As a teacher, though, it would make your life more difficult if your students saw you. And what was he doing lurking around the copy shop, anyway? Watching someone? Stalking someone?

Tommy Stokoe was in the office. I've noticed him there often after hours and wondered why the security boss had to work nights; I assumed it was the same reason that the odd faculty member comes to the office on Sundays: they prefer the office to being at home.

I said, "I've got an unusual request. I've lost a teacher. He hasn't turned up for his class and he hasn't called in. And he's checked out of the place where he was staying." I told him what else I knew about Simmonds and his world. "Now the cleaner tells me he's seen him hanging around the shop in the basement. He's obviously a weirdo so I'm wondering if any of your people have reported someone hanging around after hours."

Tommy leaned over the desk, paused, then came around to shut the door behind me. "As a matter of fact," he said, "there have been a couple of reports of a character hanging around but he doesn't stand still to be questioned you think your man is some kind of creep like Worsfold?"

Stokoe was referring to a famous incident in the previous term. A Philosophy instructor named Worsfold had wandered into the women's washroom on the second floor, looked around for a stunned several seconds and scuttled out, running, as he left, straight into the arms of a security guard who had seen him enter the washroom from a long way down the corridor. The guard took him to the office where Tommy Stokoe sent for the chairman of the Philosophy department.

The explanation was simple. At our college the washrooms are identified by the letters "M" and "W" on the doors, God knows why, because unless the two kinds of washrooms are side by side then the single letter can take a moment longer to decode than the word does. Try it. Walk down an imaginary corridor and turn sharply to confront a giant "M" and see what it tells you, momentarily. Maintenance, maybe? And so it was. Worsfold, coming out of his class, on a high from having given a lecture on John Stuart Mill, needing a pee, saw the W and in his supercharged condition assumed it stood for "Washroom."

His story was accepted — it was the kind of thing security guards believe of the faculty, especially Philosophy teachers. Worsfold's only comment when the story got out concerned his astonishment at how many women were using the facility at once. "It was like the washing place by the stream in a Greek village," he said. "A place to meet and chat and look at one's reflection in the stream. Not like our urinals at all."

If you don't believe this you don't know anything about post-lecture euphoria.

Now I said, "Worsfold was confused."

"Uh-huh and dazed I would think. Okay, I'll leave a message for the midnight shift and tell them to pass it on to the morning shift: that should catch most of them."

CHAPTER FOURTEEN

THE SAME CLERK WAS IN charge of the desk at Simmonds' old hotel, but now he didn't want to talk to me. He wouldn't even look up at first, but I put on a happy face and waited, parked in front of his wicket.

He slapped the papers he was pretending to work on, pushed them to one side, swivelled his head, owl-like, and said, "Listen, buddy-boy. When the cops ask, I answer, okay? I don't need any shit. I don't want any shit. Okay? We're working on our image here. This isn't a whorehouse or a blind pig or a home for drug dealers, not anymore. A lot of the people who stay here are from out of town, and wherever they come from, Red Deer or Moose Jaw or South Porcupine, they want somewhere cheap and clean and safe, somewhere unthreatening. Somewhere nice. So what I don't want is a stream of heavies from the drug squad or the fraud squad or the vice squad looking for their clients here. Okay? So if you find Simmonds, or Johnny Tosti, or whatever the fuck he's calling himself, tell him not to come back. We don't want him."

When I was sure he had stopped, I said, "I suppose you're saying you haven't seen him. I think he may be sick."

"Haven't; don't want to. Sick? Bullshit. Your wandering boy is in some kind of trouble and we don't want him bringing it here."

"Can I ask you a question?"

He stared at me, his face white from his high temper. "What?" he said, spitting the word.

"Some time last week he lost a tooth and had it replaced right away ..."

"Did he? You expect me to know things like that about everyone who comes through the door. Shit and corruption, if I ..."

"I thought you might have noticed."

My refusal to get angry at his tone finally got through to him. "Duncan," he called.

I looked around. The same old man was sitting in his chair.

"Did you notice his tooth missing?"

No need to remind Duncan who "he" was. "Yes, I did." He pointed to his own dark orange incisor. "Right here."

"When?" I asked.

"Early part of the week. He got it fixed right away."

"The next day?"

"Couple of days. Three. I asked him what it cost; he said he didn't know. He had a plan, he said."

"A dental plan? Insurance? You still get a bill even on a plan, don't you?"

"Probably just said that to shut me up, thought it was none of my business. He got a good tooth, though, good as the others."

"He didn't tell you the name of his dentist, I suppose?" I asked.

"Good Christ!" Behind me the desk clerk sucked air through his own teeth. "Will you kindly fucking take ...," he began to say as Duncan replied, "No, but it was someone local. He said his own dentist couldn't take him, so he looked up one in the neighbourhood."

I BOUGHT A MAP AND found a coffee shop and made a list of the side streets. I borrowed a Yellow Pages and ran through the dentists. I found fourteen. Now I made up my own list arranged in the form of a little walking tour, rehearsed my story, and set off.

I started at the corner of Wellesley and Church. I had one dentist listed on the second floor of a building near the subway. I said, "I'm looking for a friend of mine who may have been a patient of yours sometime last week. His name is David Simmonds, but he may be calling himself Johnny Tosti."

She stared at me hard, quite rightly. I hadn't thought it through.

"Let me start again," I said. "A friend of mine had a tooth fixed last week. After that, we lost track of him. I'm trying to find him."

She reached for a Kleenex, one of those people who reach for a Kleenex before they do anything. "Why don't you keep track of your friends? Or, better, why do you?"

I had an inspiration. "The point is, the man is bipolar, you know, schizophrenic, and he may have forgotten to take his meds. He hasn't called any of us lately. We're worried."

"Who's 'we'? Some kind of support group?"

I caught at it gratefully. "That's it. We keep tabs on each other. Bipolars without family. Actually you could call *us* his family."

"If you want," she agreed. She reached for another Kleenex and polished a little area of her desk that had grown dull as we talked. "So your friend — what's his name, by the way? David Simmonds? Johnny Tosti? Which? Does he know? Okay, your friend went for a walk to get his tooth fixed. What did he have done?"

"Some kind of replacement."

"Implant? Cap? Bridge?"

"I don't know."

"He didn't come to us."

The door behind her opened and a masked and rubber-gloved

man in a white coat came out and said something close to her ear, the way dentists tell their receptionists how much to stick you for. She gestured at me. "Dr. Letts, this gentleman is looking for a friend of his who had a tooth replaced last week."

"Not by me," he said.

"That's what I told him."

"I referred two implants the week before, but nothing last week."

"Thank you," I said. "I'll keep trying."

"Was it an implant?"

"What?"

"Was it an implant, or a reconstruction?"

"I don't know."

"Did the tooth break off below the gum line, or above?"

"I don't know."

"Had he had a root canal?"

"I don't know."

They both waited now for me to make sense of my story. I said, "Actually, I was away when all this happened. I'm just offering to help find him."

"You should ask your friends what kind of tooth repair he needed. It would make it easier for you."

"I'll find out. Thank you."

I TOOK MY LIST BACK to Starbucks to rethink my strategy. If every call took half an hour it would take me several hours to get around to them all, and it was already three o'clock. The solution, of course, was a telephone survey. I used the endpapers of my copy of *The Odyssey* to compose a pitch:

"My name is Joe Barley. I'm an administrator at Hambleton College and I'm presently trying to track down one of our instructors who may have suffered a temporary loss of identity. His name is David Simmonds, but he sometimes thinks he is Johnny Tosti. I understand you are his dentist and I know he broke a tooth last week, so I wondered if you had treated him, and if he said anything to you that would help me find him. Oh, he's not your patient? Sorry, I was misinformed."

I liked my "temporary loss of identity." It covered everything from amnesia to having had his soul snatched by aliens.

I gave the stunningly beautiful Asiatic child peering at me through the glass bell of her biscotti collection two toonies to change into sixteen quarters. I figured that, with the two quarters I already had, my luck would have to be very bad if I didn't find the right dentist before I needed more money. It occurred to me that maybe now it was time I got myself a cellphone — something I had been resisting so far, hoping one day to be the only one left not talking to himself as he travelled the city.

I got him in six. "Yes, he's our patient. I was away myself last week so why don't you come in and talk to Doctor Laweh. Sure, we're here until five thirty."

I had no idea what I was going to ask the dentist, just, did he have any ideas himself? Did he pick up any hints as he was rootling around in Simmonds' mouth? My dentist always asks me about my holidays. We chat away about possible vacations as if I net twenty big ones a week and have trouble spending them, like him, and then he goes in with the drill. He must pick up a fantastic amount of information about places to go, things to do, in the course of a week.

I took my time finishing my coffee, staying in the coffee shop long enough to be joined at the table by a guy carrying a typescript, sighing like a lover. "Agents," he said, throwing his hands up a little in despair as he spread his stuff around the table before settling down with his latte. "Shit on agents, I say, don't you? My agent just told me my book is out of date. How would she know? She's still wearing khaki and black. I'm really trying to weave a timeless mixture of voices, actually a collage. She says it makes for slow reading."

I stood up. In case it looked rude, I said, "Sorry, I just came in for the coffee."

He wrinkled his brow slightly, made as if to speak, then waved his forefinger. "You're excused," he said.

CHAPTER FIFTEEN

THE DENTIST HAD HIS OFFICE on Isabella. I turned the corner off Church and crossed the street. I started looking at the numbers of buildings; but, before I got too far, I saw something familiar from a block away, the side view of Constable Sargent leaning against one of those so-called unmarked cars, the kind that scream their official status by their lack of bells and whistles and any other exterior adornment. (The convention of the "unmarked car" always reminds me of the convention of classical drama, that a disguise that is meant to fool the people on stage is transparent to the audience. An "unmarked car" allows the cops to pretend they are invisible, though to the kind of citizens they are pursuing they might as well be naked.) Sargent was obviously waiting for someone. I did a rough count of numbers and guessed that he was outside the dentist's building, and from this it was a small step to guessing that he was planning to cross my path. But why?

Having been warned off once, I didn't want to risk irritating him so I crossed the street to go around the block to my car. I assumed he was there courtesy of the dentist's receptionist, and that he had got there by following a similar track to mine as far as the dentist's door. By now the dentist would have been instructed to tell me nothing.

And then, as I was wondering what to do next, I was overtaken by a desire to go home. I was sick of it, all of it: of Simmonds, most of all, but also of Hambleton. I had a pregnant partner and no job, and any time I spent looking for Simmonds should be spent filling out application forms.

"Hello again," the man with the typescript said, in my ear. "Still not looking for someone?"

"Just loitering," I said. I patted his arm and headed for my car.

THAT NIGHT WE GOT DAUBE d'Avignon, followed by a kind of pear tart with quince syrup and vanilla-honey ice cream. Recently we had had Vealburgers a la Wallenberg, as served in the opera house in Oslo; a very special minestrone using a recipe a friend had obtained from a restaurant in Lucca; and a frittata made with shrimp, chili peppers, and Parmesan cheese, courtesy of Jamie Oliver. Everything was delicious and all a surprise. The only contribution I made was Swedish meatballs Ikea, and they were good, too.

As far as I was concerned we could go on like this forever, although I knew we couldn't. I said, "I'll clean up the kitchen."

THE MEETING BEGAN AT TEN. A reply had appeared, headed "The Real Argument from Authority." In it, the "Business Instructor" quoted figures from a recent article in the local press, figures that showed how keen the leaders of business (the real authority) were on hiring M.B.A.'s. Seventy-eight percent of those surveyed said they would prefer to hire candidates with M.B.A.'s over applicants without the diploma. And, further to that, an accompanying article on the same page told of the huge demand for teachers of the M.B.A. Thus both "authority" and "the marketplace" have spoken, the Business Instructor said. Surely that was conclusive?

The reply came immediately in the form of another one-page special edition of *The Rag*. Entitled "Hoist with His Own Petard," the piece simply pointed out that, while seventy-eight percent was a figure that seemed to speak very loud, the really interesting figures were the fourteen percent who were indifferent, and, most of all, the thoughtful six percent of executives for whom the possession of an M.B.A. would make a job candidate less appealing. Could this happen in any other field? If the heads of teaching hospitals were asked the question, is it conceivable that six percent of them would prefer interns with no medical training?

In his reply to that (published the next day), the Business Instructor pointed out that while Business Administration was a real profession, it was not the kind that required a particular technical knowledge, like medicine or rocket science, but, rather, a wide understanding of principles, like English. In English, he understood, Hambleton required that its instructors have a Ph.D. to assure the university and the world of the high quality of its faculty, not simply so that they would look good on paper. And, as in the world of business, really distinguished minds always declared themselves, with or without diplomas; scholars like Frye or Woodhouse were the extraordinary exceptions that proved the general rule. So it was in business, he said. And — a further thought — the six percent of eccentric employers hostile to the M.B.A. would certainly contain a number whose hostility was rooted in a personal failure. Had the English Instructor not come across similar situations in his own field?

A nice crack, I thought, though coming a bit close to home

The letter ended with a neat response to the reference to Samuel Johnson's remark about "business" not being difficult. "The 'English

Instructor," the letter said, "is to be congratulated on having successfully shored up his position with quotations from the great Samuel himself," adding, "What a blessing Google is in helping us to show our learning! But if the writer had googled on a bit further, he might have come across another interesting remark of the great man, a comment about the morality of the business world, a topic English instructors are fond of discussing. The words may be Boswell's, but he is at the very least paraphrasing Johnson when he says, 'There are few ways in which a man can be more innocently employed than in getting money.'

"Thus Johnson on the morality of the business world. Not, perhaps, what English instructors unfamiliar with Boswell's work might have expected."

JACK CHEVAL IS IN HIS second year as chairman. Actually, he came in at Christmas last year to replace a man who had been chairman for only a year before he resigned because the department wouldn't agree with his revolutionary reforms. That one, Maurice Riddell, wanted to return to a classical curriculum of literature at least fifty years old, to have us teach nothing published after 1945. It was the program he ran on (we elect our chairpersons), but we only elected him because the alternative candidates were unthinkable and we didn't believe he was serious. He was, though.

Jack, then, took over at Christmas, and decided to run the department as if he were the boss. Now, all meetings start on time whether anyone is there or not. Jack can rattle through an agenda getting approval from those present and be back in his office ready to turn law into action in about a quarter of the time it used to take. The "I object" crowd becomes hysterical, of course, but since they are not the most popular people in the department, Jack always gets his own way.

Normally, the temporary faculty are not present at department meetings. Today he invited me to join the group as a non-voting member, because he had decided after all to raise the problem of the identity of the letter writer with the whole department. I thought I might have to sit outside the door until the item came up, but Jack said the meetings of the department are closed but not secret. In fact he reminded me that in a previous scuffle the sessionals and other part-time peoples had won the right to have an observer at these meetings, as long as we didn't speak.

Jack called the meeting to order at 10:05, introduced me, or rather, explained my presence, and went through the litany of other business before we got to the agenda proper.

The first item concerned the fainting room, a room with a couch, adjacent to the ladies' washroom. Lately we have been so short of space that the department secretary had been obliged to store some office supplies in this room, which meant that male members of the faculty needing copy paper had to find a female colleague to get it for them. Giles Bainstock, an elderly Englishman, said it reminded him of his father's stories about growing up in England when children used to stand outside cinemas asking someone to take them in if the film had an "A" certificate.

Jack said he would sort it out, and we moved on to the next item, a request from the faculty for permission to use our own offices on statutory holidays. This was a perennial item, and Jack tabled it until he could get the opinion of the security people.

It went on like this, nothing curricular — that's all dealt with in the spring — and nothing to do with money, sabbaticals or hiring, or travel grants for conferences, all of it dealt with in "committee of the whole" — i.e., out of the sight of people like me. Eventually we came to me, under "A.O.B."

Jack said, "Close the door."

The door was already closed, but I got up and rattled it a bit. It was obvious that Jack was preparing us for something important, and I expected a speech, with a beginning, middle and end, and a joke or a light remark to start us off.

Jack said, "Now then, who wrote those fuckin' letters."

It was a bad sign. Unlike the English fox-hunting classes, Jack doesn't leave off his final G's unless he's very agitated.

The only clue I had so far had come from my friend Boris's linguist, who had identified a couple of distinguishing hiccups. The first was the use of the word *round* instead of *around*, as in the phrase, "he lived round the corner." "Round," says Boris's linguist, is British; "around" is American. News to me. I tested it in my head a couple of times and it seemed true enough at first hearing and then the certainty faded as I pressed the word, rather like the childhood experience of having words lose their meaning if repeated often enough late at night in bed.

The second example was intriguing. The anonymous letter writer had said, as part of his attack on the standards of literacy in the business world, that the correspondence of one C.E.O. he knew sounded as if the executive had consumed a half-bottle of rye with each letter. He, the writer, had made a profitable sideline out of correcting all this man's correspondence before it left the office, in fact before his secretary saw it. The use of email kept the drafts private until they could be corrected, and the slowest turnaround was overnight. Thus the C.E.O. had developed a reputation on Bay Street for the elegance and pithiness of his prose.

Not to brag, but it sounded a bit like the early days of my relationship with Herb Mullins. Nevertheless I didn't believe a word of it. It seemed so pat and invented, so much polished in the telling, it had all the feeling of invention and little of the smell of truth. But true or false, it was very revealing. As the linguist pointed out, the phrase "a half-bottle" is British. A Canadian would say "half a bottle" but even then, only if he intended to mean half of a once-full bottle. What the Brits call a half-bottle, Canadians call a mickey. And the fact that the letter writer had added "of rye" confirmed (for the linguist) his Britishness, because the British don't drink rye and thus the writer was trying to throw dust in our eyes by drawing attention to his (false) Canadianness.

I'm thinking of contributing a paragraph or two about all this to the next *Canadian Notes and Queries*.

There were twelve people in the room, and I focused on the two Englishmen and Betsy Blue, my liking for whom was slightly qualified by the small smile that sometimes played about her lips, nearly a smirk, which made me want to assess the foolishness of what I had just said. Apart from these three, we had six Canadians and an American. None of the Canadians is Anglophile enough to affect a British syntax — those people are all in the History department — so it looks as if the letter writer, if he is in the department, is Giles Bainstock or Martin Love. Bainstock I set aside simply because the man is so well-balanced, essentially sane and with a sunny temperament, a man who finds humour in everything but is never malicious, whereas this letter writer has a sharp edge to him (or her), sharper than Giles has ever shown. And Giles might think it fun to tease the Business department, but he would sign his name to anything he wrote.

Martin Love, on the other hand, is perfectly capable of writing a letter in a concealed hand, but in this case he would have had to be in a very genial mood to express himself so temperately. He is a sour, fault-finding Welshman, a nuisance who believes himself superior to his circumstances, Hambleton College, and he is contemptuous of us, his colleagues, even of Henry Webster, whose Ph.D. includes some knowledge of Old Norse. Love boasts — and I mean boasts — a D.Phil. from Oxford and an undergraduate degree from Cardiff. What identifies him, though, is that as a Welshman he thinks Dylan

Thomas is overrated. His own specialty is the verse of Swift.

Love's appearance bears out the Dickensian principle that villains should look like villains. He is bloated and scrofulous-looking, and when he thinks people aren't watching he has the charming habit of taking out his upper plate and wiping the scum out of the trench with his handkerchief. He applies for all travel and research grants and for extra study leaves beyond his earned sabbaticals. He is usually turned down, so he believes there is a conspiracy against him, and there is.

The main trouble with the possibility of Martin Love as letter writer is that though there is an element of waspishness in the epistles, the writer is evidently having fun. The poison that runs through Love's arteries would dry up any light-heartedness of that kind.

As for Betsy Blue, I made a note to ask Boris's linguist if a South African academic would express herself in British speech patterns, and set her aside to wait for his reply. I could see no other obvious suspects.

Jack was saying, "... and the president has got his Y-fronts in a twist over the slurs on the college's advertising. He wants these letters to stop, please. As for me, I would remind us that realpolitik dictates that we should keep our heads down. Whoever is writing the anti-English letters is providing the whole college with the ammunition it will use when it comes to the annual sharing out of the resources. Let's face it, there are factions in this room, people who agree with parts of these letters, not so? What I'm asking is that we have our fun in private for a while. Let me remind us that three years ago we had ten part-timers. Next year we will have one, Joe, possibly. After that the rest of us will find out how solid our tenure is. 'All for one and one for all' will turn into 'Pull the ladder up Jack; I'm in.' We've shrunk more than any other department in the Arts division in the last ten years, and we have lost two of our champions. We used to have the Dean of Applied Arts on our side because she was hoping we would give her daughter a part-time job, but she's retired now and the wind in that quarter is blowing cold. We once had a friend on the Board, a senior academic from the university across the street whose son attended Hambleton because he couldn't get in anywhere else. That boy is gone now, and so is his father, and we have one fewer shield against the winds of change.

"I started this item by wanting to know who among you wrote these letters, because one of you must have. But I've got myself in a temper now, and if the culprit confessed at this point I would do or say something silly. So let me just say, stop it, now. Let's get on."

There were shrugs, headshakes, some irritation, a few looks of self-righteousness, but no one looked actually guilty.

Betsy Blue spoke. "Tell us, Jeck. What's Joe's role in all this? What's he here for? Speak, Joe. Speak."

Jack said, "Christ I nearly forgot. Joe. Yes. First, Joe is looking for help on a couple of things. I've asked him to take a look at the situation we've just been talking about to see if anything strikes him. I need someone to talk to, you see, and everyone else is suspect."

"Oh, dear. Ace Detective Barley is going to solve it, is he? The Hambleton Dick?" Love's face was one gigantic sneer. "There is no chance, of course, that he wrote the letters? He is, as we know, unreasonably embittered, believing himself entitled to a position for which he is not qualified, and his politics are the knee-jerk left-wing "my-party-right-or-wrong" kind that gave us that calamitous NDP government. I would have thought our Joe was most likely." He smiled to pretend he was joking.

When you've got tenure, and you're a shit, you can talk like that. I had the next best thing to tenure — the certainty that I wouldn't get it. We had been rude to each other before, Love and I: if this had been some other world, I'd have been across the table to teach him some manners, but this is academe and I'm not a fighting man, anyway, so all I said as I unfolded myself from my chair and made my way to the door was, "Stick it up your ass."

Jack put his hand on my shoulder to push me back down. "On the other hand," he said, "I asked him because the style of the letters, florid and poncey, is not his style."

"Who has a florid and poncey style?" Betsy asked, catching Jack's drift immediately and looking around the room with that wide-eyed look that clever women use when they are feeling wicked. "None of us, surely?"

Everyone except Love knew right away whom she meant. Then Love did, too.

Jack quickly charged back in before there was blood on the floor. "I have to tell you of a couple of developments before we go ahead."

He was interrupted by Betsy. "Do you have any suspects, yet, Joe? It must be one of us, you think? It's like that Agatha Christie novel. I mean perhaps you'll find a way to eliminate us one by one — metaphorically, of course — until it will turn out that the villain is Jeck. Eh, Jeck?"

Everyone tried to smile but a lot of them looked uneasy at the idea of an investigation. Jack waited, pointedly ignoring Betsy, and then resumed.

"First of all, there is a lot of interest in this business. Some of it is just clever students enjoying themselves at our expense, asking us which party we belong to, the structuralists, or the deconstructionists, or whatever. What is trickier is that I have heard of some students beginning to question the validity of their last semester's grades, and asking if the papers should be reread by another instructor. Be ready for that one, and if I have to respond, don't come to me with any nonsense about no one else being qualified to assess your students, because I'll find an outside examiner if I have to. I presume that none of you will claim that only you know what you know?

"Now, on this matter of outside examiners; fortunately, at a dean's meeting yesterday, I recruited some allies in the faculties of History, Philosophy, and Political Science, none of whom see the need for outside examiners here, yet. Economics and Geography don't care, interestingly enough. Perhaps they aren't true arts subjects. At any rate, we aren't alone in this."

Silence for a few minutes, then a question here, a response there, several voices together, blended into a parliamentary uproar as the department members reacted out of their different concerns.

Betsy said, "Isn't this rather an excessive reaction, Jeck?"

Jack said, "I'm trying to be proactive. My idea is that when we are attacked separately, we should respond from a shared position. In the meantime, if I can't know who wrote those letters, let me assume they were written in a spirit of fun, and now they will stop. Okay?

"But this wasn't the only reason why I asked Joe to join us. Say your piece, Joe. No, before you speak, let me tell the rest of you what I want you all to do about these letters. I would like Joe to take the lead in helping us to nail this bugger and shut him up. Or her. But Joe needs your support, so I'll make a motion. I move that Joe be asked to look at these letters to see if he can get a handle on them and that he be given the freedom to do whatever is necessary to find out. All those in favour?"

The vote was eleven to Love.

"Good," Jack said. "Up you get, Joe."

I said, "Just to finish the last item, if any one has any ideas, would you tell me? All gossip, rumour, innuendo gratefully accepted. But, yes, the other reason I'm here is to request your help ... no, actually just tell you, about another matter.

"I assume you all know that one of the part-time people has disappeared. David Simmonds, who has been teaching Business Correspondence in the evening program for the last two months, didn't turn up for work last week and again this week. There has been no word from him or of him, except from one of his students who claims to have seen him, wearing a disguise, in a downtown coffee shop. I'm afraid there is a possibility that he may be mentally disturbed. I checked on his home address, which I found was a cheap hotel on Jarvis Street, and learned he's been living there under a different name, but he's gone now. There are a couple of other odd things. I've just learned that the SIN number he gave us belonged to a street person who died of exposure eleven years ago. Simmonds checked out of the hotel the day before he was supposed to teach his class. I've talked to the police in case something has happened to him, but they say they have no report of him. Rumours may start. *The Hambletonian* is bound to send out a student to practise on a story like this. The thing is, we know hardly anything about the guy. I thought someone here who has a class in the extension division might have exchanged a few words with him. If so, did you get any idea of the man? His academic qualifications are phony, too, by the way, but he was evidently teaching Business Correspondence well enough and the students would be sorry to lose him. I've taken over his class for the moment.

"The guy is an imposter and may be out of control. If you do see him, be sure he wants to see you before you rush over and shake his hand. Please tell Jack or the police. Now having said all that, I think it would be a good idea to play it cool, to keep the whole thing within the department. It won't help to turn it into a news story. That's my advice."

In the course of my speech, I believe I caught the eye of everyone in the room long enough to draw a complete blank, as far as guilt or knowledge was concerned.

Betsy said, "Why not tell you, Joe? Why Jeck or the police?"

It was the question I had been working towards, the announcement of my last hurrah.

I said, addressing myself to Jack, "Because this is not my pigeon. If you want Simmonds found then you have to hire someone to do it. My former agency would supply someone. Five hundred a day they charge. I've done everything necessary so far, and the police are informed. I'm intrigued by this guy, sure, especially with the disguise gimmick and all, but for myself, I don't feel like working *pro bono* Hambleton. I need some adequate incentive, if you know what I mean, like money."

This was the first time I had organized my new thoughts, even to myself, but they had been growing for a while so the speech came out fairly coherent. I was pissed off. Asking me to worry about Simmonds on my own time was typical of Hambleton if not of Jack himself, and it was not on.

Everyone in the room knew that something important was happening in their tiny cosmos, if not just what; they waited for Jack to respond.

Jack said, "I think that's very clear, Joe, and put like that it's very understandable. Does that go for finding the letter writer, too?"

"No, if you don't mind, I'll still look for the letter writer. I'm very curious about him.... Or her." I smiled around the room.

"We'll all be happy to see you find the bastard, Joe. All right. You all heard: if you see Simmonds, tell me. If you have any ideas about the letter writer, tell me and Joe, too."

The meeting broke up, but before I could leave, Timothy Cotter caught my sleeve. We left the room together under his silent direction. Outside, he said, "So that's what you were doing the other night? I was thinking of outing you."

CHAPTER SIXTEEN

I SAID, "ME? YOU THINK I was cruising?"

"Shsh," he said with elaborate fake-warning gestures. "Not so loud! I was just joking. No. So you were looking for the missing instructor, were you? Is that his manor?"

"Manor?"

"Thieves' and politicians' slang for 'territory,' Joe, probably out of date now." He looked at his watch — a half-hunter, I think they're called — which he carries in his top jacket pocket with a little strap to reach to his buttonhole.

"Now?"

"I have a class at twelve. Let's go."

It's fun to watch Timothy keep his charm in shape by performing simple tasks like bewitching the pants off the elderly Hungarian woman who pours coffee, catching the cleaning woman by the elbow to lead her to wipe down a table for us, nodding all the while to half-a-dozen customers. He has the world in his pocket, and if he ever runs for office he'll win in a walk.

"You've made yourself at home here," I said, when we were seated.

"It's what I've learned to do," he said enigmatically. "I even managed it in Scrod Harbour. A friend of mine used to run a little sort of coffee shop down in the harbour, and I helped out from time to time. I got to know all the fishermen. I'll tell you one thing, whenever I gave a dinner party I served the freshest fish my guests had ever had. Have you ever tasted cod that is only an hour out of the water? Those fishermen are the only people I miss from my previous life. Now, what can I do for you? How is Carole, by the way?"

The guy took my breath away. As a department, we don't go in for much formal jollification, and with the exception of a couple of part-timers — now gone, of course — and Costril, a former part-timer and friend, now a tenured person I avoid, no one has met Carole. They know she exists, but she has never appeared around the college, seeing no reason to trek out to our neighbourhood in the east end of the city. But last spring, after only nine months in the department, Timothy invited us, sight unseen, as it were, to a little dinner party where we were joined by two chaps from Theatre, a man-and-wife couple from History, and Timothy's current partner, a morose chartered accountant who works for a bank: a nicely balanced group.

At some point I had asked his partner — Derwent, his name is — where he and Timothy met, and the question puzzled him. He blinked at me a bit, then said, "In the neighbourhood."

The apartment they share in Rosedale occupies the second floor of a very large house. It is vividly furnished, full of copies of interesting objects and hung about with swathes of curtaining. Japanese pornographic prints decorate the bathroom. It had been Derwent's apartment before Timothy arrived, and they were now contemplating something larger so that they didn't have to share friends all the time.

Timothy was very attentive to Carole that evening; she enjoyed herself hugely, and agreed that we must entertain Timothy sometime. Saying goodbye, and feeling the need to compliment him (we'd already swooned enough about the wonderful meal) I told him how striking I found the décor.

Timothy roared with laughter. "Don't give me credit for this poofter's palace. It's all Derwent's. It gives him release from the tensions of debiting and crediting."

"Carole wants us to get together," I said now, as we sat down.

"When?"

Timothy isn't someone you can do that "we-must-have-you-up-to-dinner-sometime" shit with — a mantra an American teacher of French I know says is peculiarly Canadian. Fortunately with Timothy, Carole means it.

"Very soon." I scratched around. "The thing is, Carole is feeling too lethargic for entertaining — she's almost due— but you'll be the first people we'll invite to view the new arrival. And to eat dinner."

"I'll come over and cook it if you like."

(I remember the way he had greeted the first news of Carole's condition.

"Carole thinks she's pregnant," I had said, "And she's afraid if people know then we will be talking about nothing else for the next six months."

He pushed back his chair and half rose in excitement. "Carole? Pregnant? That's wonderful." Pause. He sat down. "Isn't it?

"So they say."

"Jesus! Carole's going to have a baby and you don't know if that's wonderful?"

The emotion was strong, but I wasn't sure why. We didn't know the guy that well. Was it babyhood that was moving him? Recently we had dinner with a couple of gay men Carole knows from the government offices where she works, one of them a deputy minister. They told us about another couple they knew, one of whom had found a woman willing to give birth to a child for him, evidence of a desire for fatherhood much more powerful than any I'd noticed among my hetero acquaintances. Maybe Timothy had been saying it was all so easy for us.)

Timothy said, "If and when you do get around to a dinner invitation, you will probably not have to set a place for Derwent."

Very delicate ground, this. A remark like that, in a different context, would normally invite a question, but Timothy did not seem to be opening himself for a discussion. I tried for a remark that would allow Timothy to close off the topic, or continue it. I said, "Is Derwent going into seclusion? Writing a novel, maybe?"

"I don't know. Derwent isn't speaking."

"At all?"

"At all."

It seemed like time to let him return to the topic of when we might want to have him for dinner. I said, "I'll remind Carole tonight and make her fix a date. Look, help me out on this other thing. Let me tell you the whole story." I recounted all the evidence I had uncovered that Simmonds/Tosti might be well-known in the Cumbrae Meats district, adding that I was just idly curious now, having no intention of pursuing the thing any further.

"You mean, maybe he's gay?" Timothy whispered, clowning now.

I decided to ignore his play-acting. "An old man in the lounge of the Jubilee Hotel says he isn't," I said.

"Old Jake?"

"You know him?"

"I stayed there for a couple of days once, before I moved in with Derwent. Yes, I know him. His receptors are pretty feeble these days, but he's probably still trustworthy on that. Did he tell you anything else?"

I recounted my experience with the desk clerk and Old Jake.

"Yes, that hotel wants to go up-market, even attract Americans,"

Timothy agreed. "They have filtered out most of the sordid element, but they haven't attracted too many Buffalo burghers yet. That's spelt with an 'h.' Do you want me to talk to the desk clerk? And old Jake? I'm surprised he's still there."

"Would you?"

"Sure. Look, why don't we have dinner tonight, in the neighbourhood. The Dark Room on Wellesley. It's not too gaudy and they know how to make risotto. I'll talk to Old Jake first, and that bitch behind the desk, too. Okay?"

"I'd appreciate it."

"Good. Now to my point. Am I right in assuming you really want no part of finding Simmonds? Let me put it another way: you really don't intend to look for him anymore?"

"That's right."

"Do you mind if I do? Look for him?"

"You? Why?"

"I think I'm better equipped, so to speak, to find someone in the Cumbrae Meats district."

"But why? What do you care?"

"For Mr. Simmonds personally, nothing. I would be doing it for myself, you see."

"Why?"

"Oh, mind your own fucking business. When I'm ready, you'll be the first to know, but at this stage I'm feeling shy, okay?"

"You ? Shy?" And then I thought I saw. "Timothy, are you planning to go into the business, become a private investigator? I should warn you —"

"Oh, Christ, no. All right. Between us, then. Okay. I want to write a detective story. I've tried writing a novel and it didn't work. I didn't have any trouble writing: I just couldn't stop. I wrote about three hundred pages of these people talking to each other about their inner lives before I gave it up. I did some poetry in my youth, and finished the first act of a play. I imagine the record is pretty common in an English department, but what I've got out of it is that, having failed to write something important, I want to try something unimportant, because I have found I like writing. So what could be more unimportant than the mystery novel? And besides which, I think it is possible to study the genre and imitate the form while satisfying one's creative needs in the interstices of the plot with little bits of literary writing. And, too, though gay crime writers are popping out of the closet, so far as I know Toronto doesn't have one so I will have the field to myself. I will be 'the first to burst into that silent sea,' so to speak. And by a happy coincidence, with your permission I could begin my research in my own backyard. Yes, I'd like to try my hand by seeing if I could track down our man Simmonds."

He had stopped talking playfully, and as he finished, he looked away from me, his face tight and slightly sweaty as if he expected to be made fun of.

I said, "To begin with, don't do too much research. Have you got a plot?"

"Except for the disappearance of Simmonds, no."

I said, "'Three or four families, living near each other ...'"

"What?"

"Jane Austen, giving advice on the way to start a novel. Sounds to me that you don't need advice. All of what you are saying makes sense. Good luck."

"It doesn't sound silly?"

"Of course it does. It's one of the reasons writers never tell people what they are working on, because it sounds silly. It also sounds possible."

"Now, Joe, please, not a word."

"Not even to Carole?"

"Not yet. I'll tell her myself."

"So you want to get your feet wet by finding Simmonds?"

"It does sound silly, doesn't it?"

He spoke sharply, out of the shyness, no doubt, and I decided, why not, at least Constable Sargent won't recognize him. "Not to me," I said. "Are we still having dinner tonight?"

"Stay in the college until six. I'll call you later in the day and confirm the time. And then we can also fix the day that you and Carole are having me over for dinner, okay?"

I HAD DEVELOPED THE HABIT of calling Carole daily while we waited for D-Day. I did so now, telling her I wouldn't be home for dinner, and making a little anecdote of having coffee with Timothy, and inviting him for dinner.

She said, "Braised rabbit and that new rice pudding I've found. That's what I'll make him."

"If you say so."

"And fried pickerel cheeks for starters. But soon, Joe."

"How soon?"

"Any day. I've bought two cellphones so that I can get you wherever it happens."

THE DARK ROOM WAS HUMMING when I arrived at seven. It was a large open space, used later in the evening for dancing, with a bar at the back of the room, and a few tables for dining in one corner. The walls are decorated with old cameras and early photographs.

When I walked in, the main floor space was fairly crowded with pairs and small groups meeting and greeting at the end of their day. I walked over to the bar. The barman smiled. "Are you Joe?" He put his hands together, prayer-like. "He's been waiting for you. He asked me to watch out for you. He's over there."

Timothy waved at me from a table. When I reached him he called the waiter over. "Jeremy, this is Joe, and we are having a meeting. I don't want to be interrupted by people trying to join us, so would you mind taking away the other two chairs and the cutlery?" He turned back to me. "Now, Joe, put your eyes back in and pay attention. This is just a bar. From the look on your face you were expecting a bathhouse. We can go to one later, if you need the experience, but you wouldn't feel at home. Hank, this is private." (This to a young man who had braved the absence of spare chairs to stand by the table.) "My friend didn't come here to meet you." Timothy turned back to me. "Okay. The first thing you should know is that Old Jake thought you were the police and so didn't trust you with Simmonds' secret, if he has one. He says he has no idea if Simmonds is gay or not. I, on the other hand, have since made a lot of inquiries, trawled the neighbourhood, you might say, but found no one who had seen or heard of our man hitting on anyone — I had Simmonds' picture, remember. Now, here is the important bit, a couple of them thought he might be someone who had tried to buy some pot from them. This was a few weeks ago, and he hasn't been seen lately, so presumably he found a source, not hard these days."

"So he wanted to buy some pot? No big deal."

"No, but here's your problem. If he's straight, why come around here for his supply? Dealers are very careful of strangers."

"Could it be that he was just coming out? Crossing over? That what your friends remembered was someone who was trying to get picked up? I mean, how would he go about it? Trying to buy pot seems like a way to open a conversation."

"Say you so? If that's the case and your friend was really trembling into bloom, then it's possible that something nasty has happened to him."

"Like what?"

Timothy said, "Like being kicked to death by citizens unknown." He waited until he was sure I understood. "It happens, and it happens too much. Even you must have read about it." He made a gesture of impatience. "You know what I'm talking about."

"My impression of Simmonds is that he didn't seem to be a delicate plant. He looked like someone who could handle himself in most situations. In a klutzy sort of way, that is."

"Want me to write the other script? There was a gun around at some point, you said."

"He was a hooligan? Rough trade? He didn't seem like one," I said. "It doesn't make a lot of sense. Did the desk clerk have anything to say?"

"He was sure the cops were looking for your boy. They came to pick up the gun."

"So we have a guy on the outs with the law, looking for dope."

"Who's disappeared? Don't forget how this started. What was his other name?"

"Johnny Tosti."

"You have a picture of Johnny? Not Simmonds; Tosti."

"No. Simmonds is bald except on the sides and he has a moustache. I never saw him in Tosti kit."

"Gotcha." He leaned back and looked around the room. "Now, when am I coming to dinner?"

"Just you, then? Carole mentioned rabbit. That all right? She is also currently experimenting with Italian bean stew. Would you look forward to that?"

"I like north Italian bean stew. They don't understand beans in Sicily. But I'll take a rain check until Carole is on an even keel. Oh dear, here's Derwent. He thinks I'm hitting on you. At the moment, we still aren't speaking. I mean *he* isn't. Come and sit down, Derwent. We were just about to order."

The waiter brought back a chair, and Derwent sat down in silence. The three of us ordered bison burgers in sesame seed buns. The conversation turned to teaching, Hambleton College, and student illiteracy. Derwent stayed silent for the rest of the meal.

Before I left, while Derwent was in the washroom, I asked a question I had long wanted to know the answer to. "Timothy, what is it with you and Carole? Something I might understand?"

Timothy looked sly, then he relaxed. "You think that there is some kinky attraction that depends on my being gay and Carole pregnant? Uh-uh. It's because she's one of the few people I've met around here who I can talk to about books. Most of our colleagues, yours and mine, don't read books: they study literature because they have to keep up with the critical fashions and write articles themselves if they want tenure. In my case, tenure was a condition of being hired. So when I do read someone new these days, I look forward to talking to Carole about it. It's a two-person book club. Our last choice was Jane Gardam's *Old Filth*. You read that? No? You're as bad as the rest of them."

"That's pretty insulting."

"I hope I haven't queered myself with Carole." Then, "You are going to give up looking for Simmonds?"

"Oh, yes. The hell with Simmonds. I'm going to replace him right away, and if he does reappear I'll have Jack fire him."

"Then you really don't mind if I have a go? And you will let me know of anything that might assist with my enquiries?" he added in a fair imitation of an English police superintendent as seen on *Masterpiece Theatre*.

"Okay. Dalgliesh away. But if you find him, don't bring him back to me."

"What about this letter writer. The hell with him, too?"

"Maybe, but not yet. I'll announce my little triumph when I'm ready. I have an idea."

"Who wrote the letters, you mean?"

"That sort of thing."

"Martin Love?"

"It's never the one you suspect immediately, is it? No more guesses." And then I told him the rest of my concerns. "The fact is, I'm much more interested in me than I am in him. Right now my head is full of the fact that I ought to be looking for a job outside academe. How do I do that? Where do I start? Is there somewhere I can register? What do they do in the 'real world,' — the business world, the world of labour problems. Where do the office managers that Bell has laid off go? Even so, it's not the same. I mean, you see jobs advertised — 'Wanted: office manager with experience.' You never see, 'Wanted: English instructor. Some experience of the Romantics required.'"

Although I was railing at Timothy, he knew he wasn't the object. He said, "There must be something you can do, somewhere you can go to find out where people in your position start looking. And there must be some kind of teaching somewhere. God love us, Joe, I don't know. High school?"

"No. Besides, you need a certificate."

"Community college? Night school? Supply teaching? Private school? Tutoring?"

"Dotheboys Hall? Assistant to Wackford Squeers?"

But talking helped. I felt a stirring within me, a small possibility as we talked that there might be some way of bridging the gap while I looked for a serious future. "Do I sound pathetic, Timothy? I feel pathetic. Thanks for sitting still."

Timothy said, "Not a lot of help, am I? If I think of anything, I'll let you know."

THE FOLLOWING EVENING I WAS in the cafeteria, trying to repair my soul with some of Lawrence's stories, but almost immediately I was interrupted by another visitor, Dennis Vaal, a departmental colleague, a nice man but so unassertive I could never remember his name without the mnemonic, "rhymes with Paarl."

Now what?

"David Simmonds," he said.

"You've seen him?"

"Not since he disappeared, no. But I wondered if you knew about his other activities."

"I'm trying to find out. What have you heard?" This, I saw, would be my role now — passing on information to Timothy.

"I haven't heard anything, but I think his teaching was just a whatdoyoucallit, a front."

"For what?"

"His criminal activities."

I held my breath. "Which were?"

"Pot," he said. "Marijuana," he explained.

"I know what pot is. How was Simmonds involved?"

"He had contacts."

"With whom?"

"Let me start at the beginning. You know I offer a course in Caribbean Narrative Fiction? It's an option for students in second year requiring a Humanities' course. I've been preparing it for five years and this year we finally found a way to make it viable by offering it at night as well."

"Viable?"

"Attract enough students. I've always had faith that enough students would be attracted to it one day and so it has proved. This year eighteen students signed up — seventeen from Trinidad and one from Halifax."

"Please, Dennis, could we get on to Simmonds?"

"I'm trying to tell you. I had coffee once with Simmonds before my class and I rather liked him. A change from most of our colleagues — very bluff, open sort of person. So I looked for him after that, to chat with. Then one day I was talking to him over coffee about something that happened in my class. One of my students commented on a Haitian legend, and opined that the writer must have been on *bhang*. I'd never heard the term and I thought it might have a sexual meaning so I let it go, but I asked Simmonds about it later. He told me that it was the same as marijuana."

"And?"

"We got talking about it and I told him I had never tried it, not even in a pretend way like President Clinton, and he reached into his pocket and pulled out one of those old cigarette cases you see in George Sanders' movies, opened it and showed me a little row of homemade cigarettes, and gave me one. But they weren't tobacco cigarettes, they were ganja."

"Marijuana. Pot."

"Yes."

"What did you think?

"I was amazed. It's illegal, isn't it?"

"More or less, but I think they are changing the law as we speak. Did you like it?"

"Smoking it, you mean?"

"Yes."

"I haven't tried it yet. I can't seem to find a time and place that would be private enough. It has a very distinct smell, doesn't it, and I don't want to involve my wife, or upset her. I thought I'd wait until I was up at the cottage this summer and take the boat out into the middle of the lake. When Eleanor isn't around."

I was reminded of the stories old men tell of being teenagers who carried a condom around just in case until it embossed a ring-like caste mark in the leather of their wallets.

We waited, each on the other. I said, "I'm not sure what you're asking me, Dennis."

"I thought you should know that Simmonds associated with people who supplied him with marijuana."

"You mean he knew a dealer?"

"Yes."

"I think most people who smoke pot know a dealer, and most people I know smoke pot. Everybody knows how to get hold of some dope."

"Really. Do you?"

"I haven't smoked in a long time, but if I wanted some I'd ask the students in Commerce. There are probably a couple working their way through college, dealing."

"Really? So what I've just told you about Simmonds isn't very significant?"

"Not very. But thanks. I said I wanted to hear all the gossip, however trivial."

"Would you like the roach I've got in the office. Roach, that's what Simmonds called it."

"Smoke it yourself. See what it's like. Keep up with the students in Caribbean Narrative Fiction."

He giggled. "I'll see," he said.

What the story had told me was that if Simmonds thought Vaal was corruptible, then Simmonds wasn't very perceptive.

It didn't add much to what was known about Simmonds, but I made a note to tell Timothy.

CHAPTER SEVENTEEN

THE LETTER THE NEXT MORNING took up the entire front page of *The Rag*. News of the correspondence had spread; the other two business schools in town had reprinted it all, and stories about it had appeared in student newspapers across the country, even appearing over the border, in the student newspaper of a teachers' college in North Dakota. One of our student journalists had told his English professor that *The Rag*'s editor was hoping the story would be picked up in New England, by Harvard, perhaps.

This time the "Business Instructor" had his fun with the English department's usage, as reflected in the examination question papers. He was particularly interested in punctuation, a matter of universal concern, he said, judging by the success of a couple of recent books on the subject. He wondered if the department had considered issuing a little style guide, just for the use of the university, because looking at the various styles of punctuation used in their examination papers, the English department drew on so many different traditions that guidance was needed about which to choose. About the use of the colon, for example. In looking over a handful of English exams in the spring, he had noticed several contradictory uses. Did the members of the department ever read each other's exams? And where do quotation marks go — outside the final stop, with the Americans, or inside with the Brits? From what he had seen, in the English department you could put them wherever you liked, and change your practice on every page.

The writer went on to ask for help in deciding between using brackets (parentheses) and a pair of dashes, and on the propriety of using both a question mark and an exclamation mark at the end of a sentence. On he went, pissing himself with glee, until he came to "some other small matters of grammar." One he was most perplexed by, he said, was the confusion between adjectives and adverbs. On Saturday, one of the lady columnists in the *Globe* had used the sentence, "Women, not surprisingly, felt differently." Ought that not to be "different"? he asked. It was important to be ready to defend oneself against the grammarians of Bay Street, those businessmen who are proud of knowing the two points of grammar their children don't. There are more of those people in boardrooms than academics might think, he said.

Finally, after a disquisition on the difference between "uninterested" and "disinterested" — an old hobby horse of his, he confessed, and maybe a dead one, not worth flogging — he came to his last complaint, the steady erosion of the difference between the subjective and objective case, as in, "He left his money for Mary and I to share equally." It is a solecism, he said, that is now cropping up in the prose of university presidents, including ours, and is out of hand.

I photocopied the whole thing and faxed it to Boris's linguist. I was sure we would nab the letter writers soon.

I WAS TRYING TO COLLECT my thoughts about Falstaff in preparation for my *Henry IV* class. I find Falstaff a very tricky customer to tell students about, because he seems obvious, and I can't think past that. For me, and I think most people outside English studies, his behaviour on the battlefield is unforgivable, but very familiar. It is the behaviour of Everyman when no one is watching. He is, morally, an adolescent or even a pre-adolescent. When I was thirteen I used to belong to a gang in East Kildonan who stole stuff, and if we found a car unlocked we'd have a look inside. We never broke into houses or anything; we were just shoplifters. We never got caught. Then one day I was fourteen and it stopped; that is, I grew up, realizing how much I had to lose if I got caught.

Falstaff never grows up. He's thirteen going on fifty, as everyone says. He's a coward, a braggart, a liar, a tosspot, a drunk, and a thief, like a lot of adolescents, but he is one who refuses to grow up, to leave his own Garden, the non-moral pre-adult world. In my early attempts at profundity I tried all the usual guff on students about Falstaff representing "the spirit of anarchy" or "The Underworld" in the play to remind us that he is a part of our own nature. But it's just rhubarb and the last time I tried it, Ron Crabtree's face told me so. Falstaff is no longer a part of Hal's nature: however you analyze the world of the play as "the mirror of nature," Falstaff doesn't fit.

I think Shakespeare knew all about Falstaff, having been thirteen himself once, but never bothered to chat about him, letting Falstaff's words and actions create their own little world alongside Hal's. (I have no trouble with Hal's rejection of him. It's no big deal. Hal has left the pre-moral world of Falstaff behind; he's a big boy now. I felt the same way about the kid across the street when I moved up to Grade Ten.)

I've long wanted to talk to a specialist about this, but though we've got specialists in most things we haven't got a Shakespeare person yet.

This time, for once, I didn't think about Ron Crabtree as I got ready, and then I did. But I had thought so long about Falstaff that I felt perfectly able to respond to any question Crabtree might have. If I talked about my own doubts about the more arcane interpretations of Falstaff, then all he could do would be to nod and smile. I was prepared for anything, and, thinking that, I realized once more that that was all it took to be a good lecturer — about a week's hard thought per lecture.

Timothy walked in on my thoughts. "I enjoyed our little tête-à-tête yesterday," he said. "Did you learn anything?"

"I learned something about your neighbourhood."

"My neighbourhood? I live in Rosedale. I was just entertaining a friend from the country, showing him the big city."

"Me?"

"Of course, you. One has to be careful with outsiders. They're easily ... er ... surprised."

"I thought the Dark Room was a nice little bar with a very friendly atmosphere. What's surprising about that?"

Timothy looked at me, measuring me. "Would you like to see where the natives go?"

"How about the Juggler Vain? That looks lively." I had noticed the bar on a side street. A shingle like a pub sign hung outside. A portrait of the juggler, naked nearly to the crotch, was painted on one side. The other side had a view of the juggler's back down to the cleft of his buttocks.

Timothy shook his head. "I won't take you in there. They don't like tourists."

"Tourists?"

"Excursionists from the straight world, heeding new voices. Now, what's my next move?'

"You want to stay with it?"

"Of course. It's fascinating, watching everyone with my little magnifying glass. Don't look lost: I'm speaking in metaphor. You took metaphor in Grade Eleven, surely?"

"All right, all right. Let me lay it out for you again. You're looking for a missing instructor, a man who once looked like the picture I showed you, although we now have reason to think ..."

"Oh, I like that."

"What?"

"'We have reason to think.' Makes me want to rush out and buy myself a raincoat and a trilby hat. Go on."

"Fuck off. I think the picture has changed, or rather, he has."

"So?"

"We need a new picture."

"What's your interest in him now? You want him back in the classroom?"

"I told you. I've had it with him; I've already replaced him. I'm slightly curious about the mystery now, the disappearance. Who is this guy? Where is he? What's he doing? Is he dead? Let me know when you find out, won't you?"

"I'll keep my spies asking around. He's got an earring, you say? Granny glasses, too? Can't we do better than that?"

"I've been thinking about that. Let me call you in the morning."

VLADIMIR, MY BULGARIAN FRIEND WHOSE car had been stolen, had asked me for a ride home. "Any news on the car?" I asked when he arrived at my office.

"I was in the police station two days ago, and they explained to me what has probably happened. Apparently stolen cars get shipped to Eastern Europe, or are dismantled and the parts sold to unscrupulous garages and then fobbed off on their own customers as new."

I said, carefully (because I'm never quite sure that Valadimir is not making elaborate Bulgarian fun of me), "I would think that only applies to new cars, Vladimir."

"The office cleaner said the same thing this morning. But I've found out there are lots in the city, automobile graveyards, so to speak, where old cars go to die, and amateur mechanics check these places for cheap parts when they need one for their own cars. Now there are several very distinctive marks on my car — call them dints — which I could identify, and I thought I would look around these lots and see if I could find any of my parts."

I said, "It sounds like that Italian film."

"That is where I got the idea." And he turned in his seat and smiled.

TIMOTHY APPEARED IN MY OFFICE the following morning. He said, "What we need in this story is a street photographer taking pictures on spec, and then displaying them on a rack outside his shop the next day so that the people he has snapped can order copies. You know, *Brighton Rock*."

"Those photographers disappeared about fifty years ago, in detective stories, anyway. You could prowl the streets with Starkey, the student who saw Simmonds in disguise." And then I got a glimpse of an idea. "Hang on, I've thought of a way we might fake a picture. Leave me alone now."

I took Simmonds' picture over to our Centre for Motion Picture and Still Photography. Hambleton's humble origins included a Photographic Arts department where students could train for a diploma in photography, the chief option being portrait photography. In the course of time — actually, as soon as the Dean of Applied Arts heard about it — "Motion Picture" was added to the curriculum. Within a few years it had taken over the department, and the name was changed to Centre for Motion and Still Photography. The old program still exists, but it has very few students and will soon be put out of its misery. In the meantime, the college has the usual problem of what to do with tenured faculty qualified to teach in programs for which there is no demand. (Not just in Photographic Arts. In the backrooms of Interior Design two highly skilled cabinet makers, left over from the days when the department taught furniture making, spend their days restoring antique furniture for one of the city's largest auction houses.) But the transition period is nearly over. Typing, for instance, once a mainstay of the old Secretarial Science program, has gone, along with the typewriters.

For several years Ernest Plumtre has practised his trade — what he calls "the craft of photography" to distinguish it from the "art of photography," which he holds in contempt — by attending to the institute's needs for a pictorial record of its activities. His colleague, Philip Blythe, equally close to retirement, is the one who takes the pictures. The two veterans putter along cheerfully, content even though the making of a record of Convocation that used to mean a couple of weeks' work for both men now means a video. They don't repine. They have the yearbook to produce and the calendar to supply with illustrative pictures, and they have become consultants to anyone who needs advice on choosing a camera, or help in enlarging an old snapshot.

Ernie now looked at my picture under a strong light. "Who took this?"

"I don't know. He brought it with him when he came."

"It's an unusual size. Is he a foreigner?"

I knew what he meant. Ernie was born in Devonshire sixty years ago, and he has the habit of his race of regarding all immigrants to Canada except the British as foreign.

I said, "He sounds Canadian to me."

He said, "It's just that it's bigger than our passport photos, for instance. What do you want me to do with it?"

I explained.

He said, "Run that by me again. This bloke has disguised himself, you say. Granny glasses, earrings, shaved his head. You want to know if I could produce a likeness of the new man by sketching in the changes on this picture?"

"Yes."

"And you say you've got someone to confirm what this lad should look like?"

"I can bring him in this afternoon."

"You do that, then. I've never done this before, but I've often wanted to. Let's have a go. When will you be back?"

"Four o'clock?"

"Make it three. I have to be out of here by four to beat the rush on the Parkway. In the meantime I'll enlarge this beauty to a decent size and make half a dozen copies, give us room for a bit of trial and error. I'll see what Philip thinks. Right you are. Interesting."

BACK IN THE OFFICE I called Atkinson, my boss, to ask if he could fix me and Timothy up with an interview with someone on the drug squad.

He said, "This may not be the best time. Apparently there's another investigation."

"I read about that. I don't think I'd be very threatening. The thing is, I've had a few hints that this missing instructor had some connections to the marijuana trade."

"Everybody's connected with the marijuana trade. Even my widowed sister has got a supplier. That's why the cops I know would like to see it legalized so they can get on with catching murderers and swindlers, and smoke dope in peace themselves. How's your investigation going? Got any clues?" He chose the word carefully and pronounced it heavily to show he was being funny. "I told you to leave it alone. You've got a replacement for the class. Forget about it. Move on. I've got a bit of work for you again, if you want it."

"Where did you hear I had a replacement?"

"I bumped into your security guy, Tommy Stokoe, at a retirement party for someone we both knew on the force. So move on. Forget about it."

"It bugs me."

"What?"

"Simmonds. Walking out like that. I want him caught so we can fire him."

"What's your latest move?"

I told him the idea I had for Timothy, to show a picture of the mock-up of Simmonds in disguise around the places he'd been seen.

"That's clever. Where's that? The places he's been seen, I mean."

"The gay district, the student supply shop, and the copy shop across the street."

"Jesus, how many people do you have working for you? Are you paying them?" His voice was amazed. He was trying to chuckle, but he really wanted to know.

I said, "This man has friends doing legwork for free, and Romero, our office cleaner, is keeping an eye open."

"That's it?

"And me." I kept myself in the story to help Timothy. People, I thought, were more likely to go to bat for me than for him. Some of them, anyway.

"Well, well. What was it again you wanted to know from me?"

"How the marijuana trade works. Where does the stuff come from?

Who distributes it to the dealers? How many dealers are there? Is the mafia involved? How do you get to be a dealer? What does marijuana cost an ounce? A kilo?"

"Before I answer all that, or find someone else to answer it, let's find another word, eh? You're rolling 'marijuana' around your tongue like someone learning to speak. Call it 'pot,' okay? Now what you want is all public information. You don't want specific information about the Toronto scene, right?"

"All I want to know is how it's done, not specifics about a particular case they are working on. I could probably find out most of it from Google, but I'm afraid I might miss the one essential story when I'm reading the half-million others. A quick chat with a local man is what we want. Then I'm finished with it."

"I'll see what I can do."

Half an hour later I got a call from a policeman telling me all I wanted to know about the marijuana trade, adding a warning that we might be getting close to some really bad guys, and did we want that?

I was pleased with the information, and impressed by Atkinson's connections to a force he hadn't been part of for ten years, at least.

CHAPTER EIGHTEEN

ONCE UPON A TIME, HAMBLETON COLLEGE, like a lot of colleges, invented a one-year program aimed at dropouts and late bloomers, a sort of bridge from no man's land to the regular world. Anyone could apply: all they had to do was answer a single essay question, writing five hundred words under supervision on why they wanted to get into the program. The college didn't look for specific answers; we didn't care what they said. It was how they said it that mattered. Did the answer reveal a sufficient control of grammar and punctuation to provide the minimum base they needed to resume a formal education, and did they seem like adults?

The college assumed that the program would be needed for three or four years, rather like those programs put on after the war to give veterans a chance at college. (They must have been a lively experience for the instructors. A now-retired colleague often told the story of teaching Randall Jarrell's "The Death of a Ball Turret Gunner" to a class that included a former ball turret gunner.) But the need Hambleton was responding to didn't dry up. After the flower children and the folk singers had gone, the college continued to get applications from late bloomers and dropouts from different generations, people who wanted a chance to prove they should be considered again for tertiary education. And so I came, twenty years later, to meet my English 1A class that morning.

They are the usual mixed bunch, including two middle-aged women — both New Canadians, one French and one Brazilian — neither of whom has a secure grip on the language, but both of whom make up for it by bringing other experience to bear.

The class likes it on the whole, and so do I, but I have to remind them occasionally what we are here for.

I planned today to stir up a bit of debate by bringing them two statements — Robert Frost's remark that writing poetry without rhyme is like playing tennis without a net, and Nietzche's, that the poet trying to write verse while conforming to the rules of sestinas and sonnets and so on is writing in chains. I was looking forward to thinking about the topic with them myself. And it was both easy enough for all of them to understand and provocative enough to intrigue Ron Crabtree, I thought.

But there was no chance. When I arrived they were already arguing among themselves about the story on the front page of *The Rag*, and before I could write my two quotations about the nature of poetry on the blackboard, Louise's hand was in the air. Could I please explain the problem in the newspaper, she asked. What was the difference between an adverb and an adjective?

I took a quick poll of the class to make sure they would not feel short-changed if I dealt with this, but no one seemed irritated, so I plunged right in. Ron Crabtree gave me a nod to indicate that though he had no problem himself differentiating between adverbs and adjectives he would be happy to listen to me explain the difference to the rest of them. An hour later I emerged having tackled all the problems raised by "Business Instructor" and with a request to deal with the colon next day. The question of "What is poetry?" could go on hold. It was grammar they were interested in. Still, it's nice to have a lecture in your back pocket for a snowy day.

I ARRANGED TO MEET STARKEY, the student who had seen Simmonds in his disguise, in my office where I was waiting with Timothy, and we set off to see Ernie in the Photo Arts building. Ernie had prepared a few enlargements of the picture and he and Starkey got to work. Starkey seemed to have a bit of drawing skill, and soon created a heavily worked-over portrait of Simmonds in disguise. Ernie photographed this, and the two of them worked on the result to produce a refined version. Starkey got Ernie to make one more version, and then pronounced himself satisfied with the result. He said it now looked like a picture of Simmonds in disguise after a fight, and that would do. We waited while Ernie made us a dozen copies so that Starkey could take a couple with him. "I'll show them to my friends," he said.

Timothy took four for his friends and left, and I took the rest back with me to the office where there was a message waiting for me — from Timothy. He had gone home, but he wanted me to call him when I came back to the office. When I did he insisted on meeting me at the coffee shop beside Cumbrae's before I went home.

I said, "I don't know how urgent this is, Timothy. I'm curious to know what this guy is doing and where he is, but won't tomorrow do?"

"No, this is fascinating. I've put all my buddies on the alert. I'm giving them a picture of Tosti as soon as I can. I tell you, Joe, old sport, if Tosti is gay and living the life, I'll know in a wink."

"How about if he's not gay, if he's rough trade, say, and he got a little bit out of hand."

"You mean if he's afraid he's done some damage and disappeared for his own good? If that's the case then I would have heard about it somewhere along the Rialto. Actually I am dealing with the possibility that the next unlighted doorway will show a pair of boots, a match will be struck, and there he will be, David Simmonds."

I told him about my conversation with the man from the drug squad. "I'm trying to wash my hands of this," I reminded him, "So come with me and take over."

There was a commotion in the hall; Rogero, the foreman in charge of the cleaners, rushed in. "Mr. Barley, I saw him, too. The man on your desk." He was very excited. "Him, him," he said, pointing at the picture on my blotter. "I saw him."

I took the picture from the clip, and placed it beside the original.

He said, "Yeah, yeah. I saw both these guys, this one first, now this one."

"Where? Where did you see this one?"

"Same place, near the store. And across the street by the copy shop. And getting in his car."

Now this was something. "Car? His car? You know the car? What kind? Did you get the licence?"

I expected him to say, "Big: Blue" or "Small: Black" or something equally useless, but Rogero is Portuguese, and ever since they landed in Canada he and his friends have been focusing on the cars they will buy when they get the money. "Subaru," he said. "Forester, 2002. I didn't see the licence number but I'll watch. I'll get it." He pointed at the original picture of Simmonds. "You find him?"

"It's the same guy."

He gave me a very satisfactory reaction, a long pause, a second look at the two pictures, then a sound like "Duuurrr." Then, "Yeah, now I see. That's good, eh? Now you're only looking for one guy. Better."

"I hope so. Yeah, keep your eyes open for one guy, two faces."

It was good news for Timothy's investigation that Simmonds/

Tosti was still around. If Rogero got his licence number then we might soon be able to nail him.

For what? Failing to show up to class?

VLADIMIR CAUGHT ME AGAIN ON the way out of the office. "Going my way, Joe?"

Vladimir lived on Howland, north of Dupont. It was no trouble to take him home.

"No word from the police?"

"Silent as the grave," he said. "I am thinking of buying a scooter."

I took him right to his house. "Is that the utility pole you used to hit?" I asked. A parking space had been carved out of his front yard, but it was clear from the different coloured paints left on the concrete pole that you had to be careful driving in and out. "Riding a scooter might be cold in winter," I said. "But maybe a mini?"

"Katesmark gave me a ride in his mini once. I felt like a large tourist in Greece riding on a little donkey," he said. "People stared at us at traffic lights."

TIMOTHY WAS WAITING IN THE coffee shop with Derwent and two others: one, a short cheerful guy with wide spaces between his teeth and a bristly moustache, the face of an overweight British army officer; the other was a tall wide guy, like a door, with black hair peeping out from under his shirt cuffs. I couldn't help watching the pair of them for telltale signs of camp, aware that Timothy was watching me, knowing what I was wondering about. But there was nothing familiar, and I simply added them to my list of types. It takes all sorts to make a world, Timothy's or mine.

Timothy and I are only just getting to know each other through this thing I've roped him in on, but he must have spoken favourably about me to his pals to get them to come along. None of them was exactly suppressing excitement, but there was a collective sparkle about the group, except for Derwent, that said they thought this was a lark. I hoped it would stay that way.

I said, "Did you ever see a movie called M?"

They were all nodding as I spoke, and Timothy said, "We remembered it already. Peter Lorre. Now give me some more pictures. We'll take three each — Derwent won't want any, he's staying with me. We've already divided the quarter — what a terrific word," he narrowed his eyes, "The Quarter" — and we will scout the area. Off you go now, go comfort Carole."

IN THE MEANTIME, CAROLE HAD suddenly switched gears. When I got home, she was in the kitchen trying to figure out something to eat, having abandoned the vodka risotto. She asked me if I could relish kippers, scrambled eggs made without butter, and dry toast. I said I would have a grilled cheese sandwich — two grilled cheese sandwiches, actually, since I wasn't overweight or pregnant, washed down with a bottle of Kronenberg.

And so we ate. For dessert she ate a can of mandarin oranges, spooning them right from the can, and I munched a Kit Kat. I made some coffee, which she fancied without cream, so I drank it that way, too, taking the opportunity to see if I could switch to black permanently, or until whatever was going to happen, happened, and we adjusted to a new world.

I realized that she was now eating conventionally, that is, eccentrically, in the way that pregnant women are supposed to, full of sudden needs for foods she rarely ate in the normal way. I read it as a sign that we were nearly there, and asked her about it.

She agreed. "You don't want the details," she said. "But, yes, I think we're in the home stretch."

I had a thought. "What if for some reason I don't answer the phone? I've never used a cellphone. Maybe something will go wrong."

"I'll keep a twenty-dollar bill in my brassiere — Christ, it's big enough! — and if you don't answer I'll get a cab. I'll probably do that anyway, if I'm in a hurry."

I said, "Maybe I can give someone else your cellphone number?"

She said, "The other way around. Give me someone else to call, if you don't answer. I know, I'll call Timothy."

"He'll be pleased to help."

I was right. Timothy was delighted.

CHAPTER NINETEEN

"ONE THING FIRST," BLUEBELL SAID. "Is this a joke?"

We were in the president's office: Jason Toft, the editor of *The Rag*; Herb Mullins; Richard Lownsborough, the chairman of the Business department; Jack Cheval; Bluebell himself; and me. Bluebell had called us to the meeting. I had a class, but Bluebell's secretary had told me to cancel it.

Jason Toft said, "I don't think so, Mr. President."

"Just 'sir' will do. This isn't a television show."

"Sorry, sir. No, this editorial apparently appeared in a student paper, and someone faxed it to us."

"Where is this paper?"

"Some college in Arizona, I believe, sir."

Herb Mullins said, "Where? Didn't you check?"

"I did ask one of the staff to."

"Did they? Check?"

"I'm not sure."

"And you sent it to me?" Bluebell asked.

"No, sir. I think someone leaked it, to you and everyone here."

The editorial had been waiting for me at the office that morning, sent by email. It was reprinted from *The Daily Sunset*, the undergraduate organ of the Purly Gates School of Business.

The editorial was headed, "News from Nowhere," a witty tag, an attention-gatherer for Butlerites and non-Butlerites alike. The editorial, though, was straightforward enough.

> We have just been sent a screed from a student newspaper in Toronto (not the Toronto in California, but the town in the gulag they call Canada). This missive in the form of a letter to the paper by a member of the English faculty contains a message for all of us, all students in schools of business in the U.S.A., and presumably in Canada, too.
>
> The writer argues, in summary, that business schools should be cut loose from the taxpayer to fend for themselves. It is inappropriate, he argues, for the taxpayer, especially the poorer taxpayer, to be contributing his hard-earned dollars to support the training of the rich, i.e. the students in business schools. Business education, the writer argues, is not undertaken on behalf of the general good; its sole purpose is to make money for the graduates.
>
> Because of the difficult times that always occur in this phase of the economic cycle, we've heard this argument a lot lately but there is so much wrong with it, and the assumptions behind it, that one has only to invoke the idea of free enterprise, on which principles Purly Gates is founded, and the importance for American citizens of knowing how markets work in a free society, to see it begin to crumble. But that is so obvious it is not our concern here. Our real purpose is to try to understand how such a poisonous and incendiary piece of propaganda could ever have left the desk of even a student editor. The answer is — Canada.

To understand how such a piece of propaganda got into print you have to know that its readers exist in a state of frozen socialism that preserves the communism that long ago crumbled to dust in Russia. The home of this thinking in our neighbor is the New Democratic Party, a political cabal that has already held power in three of the ten provinces (though never for long) and has been seeking for seventy years to take over the country, and, it is their stated aim, nationalize, nationalize, nationalize — industries, means of transportation, and the farms. They have already socialized medicine, with the result that there are not enough doctors in Toronto (one of the few places warm enough to make a doctor want to live there), and some towns have to beg a doctor to make an annual visit. There are long lineups for essential technical services, and citizens have to wait years or cross the border to get the treatments they need. In a word, socialism has already infected the country and it is not surprising that business is being strangled. We need to be aware of our neighbour's ideas so our young people don't get caught by them when they travel north. They are easy to refute.

We would add that in this school we are already in the situation that the writer would "condemn" us to: John Purly Gates funded this institution out of his own pocket to give a sound business and religious education to Arizona's youth. Thus he paid for their education by hard work, thrift, and risk-taking, the college motto. The story of Mr. Purly's rise to riches is well-known. We, who are his beneficiaries, will never forget it. He endowed us, with only one condition: that we preserve his name in the name of the school. And that we have been honoured to do.

"Have you had any other reaction?" the president wanted to know.

"Not to this piece, no, sir. But quite a bit to the previous debate."

Toft consulted a bit of paper he drew out of his shirt pocket. "So far we've had calls from seven student newspapers. I expect there'll be more when I get back."

Toft was trying to look bland, but he was looking so smug he seemed to have put on weight.

"Well, stop it," Bluebell said. "Right now. Stop it. Okay?" (I think he was still smarting from being identified in the previous letter as a university president who didn't know a subject from an object.) He continued. "When did you plan to publish this thing?"

"We go to press on Friday, sir."

"Well, don't. You hear me? Don't publish this letter."

"Not publish, sir? But this is a very big story — for us, I mean. What shall I say? 'The president has ordered us not to publish any more letters'? *Is* it an order, sir?"

"Yes, it is. You say you've had seven calls so far. Well, my bloody phone has been ringing off the hook."

"Who are the callers?" Herb Mullins wanted to know.

"The mayor, for one. Apparently someone sent his office a copy of this thing."

"He doesn't like our neighbours thinking he's a socialist?"

"Not that. He's not a fool. What he's really afraid of is that every liberal in the province will write to the papers about the ignorance of our American friends. Someone in his own office suggested he should give the usual reply: 'Better Red than Redneck.' Asshole. The point is he is in the middle of the annual negotiations about shipping our garbage across the border, and he wants as little anti-American chat as possible."

While this was going on, Herb Mullins slipped me a note. I broke in now before Bluebell could say something pompous. He'd done quite well, so far. "Sir, can you leave it with me for a day. I've had an insight I'd like to explore. And Jason, don't publish anything more about this until the president says so. I think I know what is going on, but I'd like to make sure. Okay?"

Bluebell looked at me thoughtfully, then at Jason who was himself looking thoughtful. Bluebell said to me, "I don't know your name, do I?"

Jack Cheval said, "Joe Barley, sir, a part-timer in my department."

"So what's going on, Joe Barley?" Bluebell asked me. "Don't keep me in suspense."

"Sir, I think it is a student prank. No, I know it is. A hoax. I'm just about to find the name of the student." I looked at my watch. "I suggest you just laugh it off — to the public generally, but to the mayor especially."

The agitation in Bluebell's face receded as he took in what I was saying and decided to go with it. Out of the corner of my eye, as they say, I watched Toft begin to look concerned.

Bluebell turned to the two chairmen. "What do you think?"

They looked at each other, off the hook, temporarily. They nodded together.

Bluebell nodded back. "All right. Meet again when Joe Barley, here, is ready. This afternoon, Joe? Two o'clock? It won't get out of hand in the meantime?"

"If it does, it'll just spill over into the saucer," Jack Cheval said.

OUTSIDE, AS WE WERE WALKING down the corridor, I said to Herb, "How did you find out that the Purly Gates School doesn't exist?" For that was the message he had passed on to me in the president's office, and with that Toft's world had started to unravel.

He said, "The Internet, of course. So what's this insight?"

"I'll fill you in later. I have a few enquiries to make first. Sorry, that's a cliché, isn't it?" I was feeling pretty close to smug myself.

Because I knew who must be behind it; I believe I had known for some time. And in spite of the total lack of ill-will in our relationship, I looked forward to telling him to his face.

Herb said, "Enjoy yourself."

CHAPTER TWENTY

IT WAS RON CRABTREE, OF course. Searching for the identity of the anonymous letter writer among the faculty, it had never occurred to me that the culprit might be a student, simply because the prose of the letters borrowed from literary sources; it smelled of other voices, other pens, an odour I assumed came from the pen of someone steeped in letters, not a great stylist himself but soaked in the rhythms and manners of his reading. But as soon as I looked beyond the English faculty — figuratively speaking — in search of someone with similar learning, to the History department, for example, and to Philosophy, where there were several faculty members whose minor had been English and could well have passed as members of our department — what jumped into my mind was not an amateur Shakespeare scholar (there is one of those in the History department) but Ron Crabtree. As soon as I thought of him I knew I had the answer. Fortunately for me, a couple of things happened that prevented me from looking totally foolish.

Crabtree had not been to my last two classes, an absence that might have concerned me but in his case was something of a relief.

Without any effort, he kept me on my toes, a strain if kept up too long; the occasional relief was welcome. His attitude to me in class from the beginning had been so genial that I did not think his absence was a reflection on my teaching. Now, though, we needed to talk, and I tracked him down to a lecture in Economics that was just ending. I waited for him outside the classroom.

The Ron Crabtrees of this world often have an acolyte, an admirer, someone not in their league, an apprentice attaching himself to the master. Where Ron Crabtree goes, there goes his follower. Ron Crabtree's disciple was a History student from Owen Sound who nicknamed himself and was called "Muggsy," after a New Orleans' musician, giving himself an identity that he otherwise lacked.

I caught Muggsy on his way out of the class and asked him where was Crabtree.

"He's in Florida," Muggsy said. "His father died last week and he flew down right away. I have his phone number there if you need to get in touch."

"He's been away for a week?"

"Yes, sir. And he'll be away for another week, at least. He has to take care of his mother. Apparently she's not coping very well."

Reader, did you ever see a movie called *Green for Danger* starring Alastair Sim? One of the jokes involves Sim, playing the detective, reading a detective story as he is investigating the current case, turning happily to the last page to confirm that he has easily worked out who the culprit is and finding that he is wrong. That is how Muggsy's information hit me; I had approached him sure of my man, deduced the inevitable, as it were, and now I learned that I was utterly wrong. I went back to my office feeling like a fool, but thankful that the gods had prevented me from sharing my discovery with anyone before I met Muggsy. Better to feel a fool than look like one.

And then, in my office, the phone rang and I learned that part of my guess was right, that it was a student, but such a student that I was glad that this time I was certain. I spoke to my caller for half an hour until I was thoroughly rehearsed. Then I set up a meeting for the next day.

COFFEE IN HAND, WE SECURED a quiet corner of the cafeteria. I wanted to gobble him down in one bite, but I also wanted to savour my meal. I began slowly.

"You must feel pretty pleased with yourself?" I said, genially enough, but there was still the echo of the familiar sarcastic admonishment to a child who has messed up in some way — set fire to the cat, cut off his sleeping granny's hair, called the fire department to send an engine — so that he ought to have taken warning, but he was feeling so pleased with himself he heard only the words and missed the tone. I smiled at him, warmly. "Jason," I said, making up my story on the spot, "I spent yesterday with a professor of language studies up at York. Professor Clapton, an Irishman by birth, I would think — though he never mentioned Joyce or Yeats once — and a specialist in the speech and prose patterns of the United Kingdom and Ireland. I've been sending him these letters as you published them because my bosses wanted to know who wrote them, especially the ones signed by the English instructor. Professor Clapton had some interesting comments — it's a fascinating field he is in. I wish I had the brains for it."

"Did he identify the writers' ... er ... habitats?" Toft was looking pleased with himself again.

"No, I did that myself, but he provided all the information."

He was startled. "You know who wrote the letters?"

"Yes, but I want to tell you how Professor Clapton helped to confirm it."

He watched me, saying nothing.

"First of all," I said. "He looked at the style. Now, for him, the last letter contained a couple of stylistic oddities, clues, if you like, and he was on to them right away."

"Do you mean you know for certain who wrote it?"

"Hold on. I'll get to it." I could taste every word of what I was going to say. "The first clue was the use of 'round' instead of 'around.'"

"What did that tell him?"

"The nationality, or the ethnicity, of the writer."

"Which is?"

"At this point in his inquiry it looked like an Englishman, or woman, of course. But one stylistic oddity isn't enough. He or she might have picked up a quirk like that while he was a Rhodes Scholar, though I don't think we've ever had one of those at Hambleton. But there were others." I went back over my earlier conversation with Clapton. "The use of 'half-bottle,' for instance, is surely a Britishism. Over here we say 'mickey.' Did you know that? Then calling it just 'whiskey' is also British. Canadians say scotch or rye, or even bourbon. And then there's the incorrect use of adverbs instead of adjectives. It's pretty uncommon to find anyone here saying 'More important, the house is up for sale ...' or some such, which is correct, and still common in the United Kingdom."

"In England?"

"In the whole of the UK. Now, once Clapton had alerted me, I found a couple myself, the use of capitals after a colon joining two independent clauses, for instance, is very common here. And the comma splice, too; an absolute no-no here, but over there you see it all the time. Suddenly it all came clear."

"The so-called English Instructor is an Englishman?"

"You'd think so, wouldn't you? So I got a bit sneaky. I showed Clapton some examples of the prose of my three prime suspects, the three instructors from England in my department. He ruled them all out on other stylistic grounds. He said they completely lacked the tone of the letter writer, whom he called a 'cute hoor' by which he means a kind of smartass. Clapton is Irish. Did I say that?"

Toft looked wary. "But you still don't know who it is?"

"Hang on now. Clapton and I looked at the other letters, the ones from the Business Instructor, and now that Clapton had alerted me to it, I could see immediately that they had something in common with the English Instructor's letters, namely that they were written with the same smartass tone. And then Clapton pointed out where he had marked up the sentences; he had identified a number of the characteristics that indicated the nationality of the writer. It was a small leap from there to seeing that these letters were written by the same person, the same shit disturber, having fun."

Toft watched me warily. "So, find the Englishman, eh?"

"Well, there was one more oddity. In fact Clapton showed me that one of the phrases showed quite clearly that the writer was a Scot."

"What was that?"

"Oh, I'm saving that for the trial, make the bastard respond on the spot." I was guessing now, of course, but it worked.

"Trial? Trial? There's nothing criminal about this, for God's sake!"

"Not a *criminal* trial. Not yet. Something in-house. But it's gone far enough. We have reached the point where it would make a wonderful story for *The Hambletonian*, at least, don't you think? Their headline might be 'HOAX' in letters about an inch high, and their story would be that *you* had been hoaxed by a brilliant anonymous student. You know how much *The Hambletonian* hates you. Especially the Journalism instructors whose classes you never attend. How's that?"

And again it worked, and, reluctantly, I had to admire the swiftness of Toft's response. The game was up and he wasted no time in bluster. He said, "Listen, I wrote those letters."

"Oh, I know that."

"How? How do you know that?"

"It was the quotation from Dr. Johnson, remember? What he was supposed to have said to a recently widowed woman, destitute except for a small printing business her husband had left her."

"All right, all right." Toft was trying to stop me, but he didn't have a chance, not now.

"You remember Johnson said, 'Do not despair, Madam, if business were difficult those who do it, could not.' That wasn't where you got it, though. You didn't get it from Boswell. You got it from an article by Calvin Tomkins in *The New Yorker*."

"Lots of people read *The New Yorker*."

"Yes, including you and me reading the same issue in the same week your story came out. You were reading it when we had our first chat. That's how I knew it was you. It's not proof, of course, it's circumstantial, but it's all the evidence *your* court will need. You're going to look pretty silly now, aren't you, when *The Hambletonian* tells the world."

"Not if I get in first."

"You mean confess? That might be best."

We were interrupted by Herb Mullins, just arrived, looking for us in the cafeteria. "You've got a problem, Jason ..."

Jason said, "I know, I know. We've sorted it out." He waved his hand dismissing it. "We'll publish the story next week, and that will be that."

I said, "I think you'd better publish something tomorrow. One of those 'This correspondence will now cease' things like the president suggested. Then think up a story to be published later about a joke that backfired, a joke editorial, maybe. You'll know how to do that. You might get away with it."

"Get away with what?"

"You've been impersonating the English department and the Business department and now you've invented a newspaper. You've made a lot of enemies, probably including the president. In due course you'd better announce the whole thing was a joke, your joke, and keep your fingers crossed."

"Is that necessary?"

Herb said. "It would be a start. People like a joke, but they like you to own up when you are caught."

When Herb had gone, I said to Toft, "How long did you plan to keep it up?"

"I hadn't got to that point," he said.

I said, "I think you're there now. Prepare yourself for a graceful exit, consistent with what I tell the president."

"Which is?"

"That there'll be a notice in the next issue of *The Rag* and later on a story, together with a statement from you."

"I'll have to think about tha'" he said.

"You do that," I said.

CHAPTER TWENTY-ONE

ROGERO SAID, "WE SEEN HIS car again."

"Where? Around here?"

"Two blocks away. Same car. He waited for an hour, maybe, then he drove off. Same thing last night."

And maybe same thing tomorrow night? "Who saw it?"

"My wife's cousin. He's a cleaner in the Film building.

"Why did he notice it? I mean, how did he know I was interested?"

"They all know. I told them."

"How many Portuguese cleaners are there?"

"Ten, twelve. Maybe fifteen."

"All your relatives?"

"Me and my wife's. Some what you call — neighbours?"

I said, "You don't happen to know Maria Argueles, our cleaning lady, do you, Rogero?"

"Maria? She cleans for you? She's my brother-in-law's sister."

Then, for no good reason, except that once, travelling in Croatia, a friend of mine asked a goatherd if he happened to know the family of the only Toronto Croatian he had met, and the goatherd did, so now I said, "Do you know anyone who fixes dints on cars?"

The thing was, I had recently borrowed the car of Carole's brother-in-law, a new Volvo, and put a tiny scratch in the side while I was parking at night. It was my scratch to fix, of course, and so far I had two quotes, one for eight hundred, and one, from the dealer who sold the car, for a thousand. The idea of paying out that kind of money, two weeks' pay, to fill in a scratch, even if I had it, made me feel ill.

Rogero said, "My wife's cousin has a service station on Harbord. His wife's brother has a body shop on Dundas West. I'll take your car to him. He's good. We all go to him."

I imagined fifteen Portuguese careering around Toronto every weekend, playing bumper cars, shouting, "Not to worry, my wife's cousin's brother-in-law has a body shop on Dundas West. He'll fix it cheap."

Rogero added, "Carlo's shop is near the Junction. Near me. I take it to him to show him. You take my car home, I take yours."

"What kind of car do you drive, Rogero?" I didn't want to find myself driving a Hummer across Toronto.

"A BMW."

"A new one?"

"Last year."

How the hell could he afford it? By cutting back on salt cod? "Then I don't want to drive it," I said. "I might scratch it and spend two years paying for the paint job."

He laughed. "It's just a car, okay? Tomorrow I'll bring my old VW for you, a shitbox, you can't hurt it no more. But you don't bring your car here? I seen you in an old Nissan van, about 1990."

"Also a shitbox, my girlfriend says." I explained about the Volvo. "Now tell me where your cousin saw this guy we're looking for."

He took out a notebook and drew a little map with a marker pen. "There."

"What time?"

"My cousin comes to work at six."

So I had something to do and I was a little nervous about how to go about it. Simmonds was clearly staking out somebody and the world he was watching was full of words like *biker*, *mob*, *Russians*, and God knows what else. I had just wanted to tell Simmonds what I thought of him, not to expose myself and Timothy and his pals to anything bloody. I was sort of relieved that Simmonds had already driven away, because it gave me time to get used to the idea that I was about to nab him.

I called Timothy now to tell him the latest developments. I told him about the talk I'd had with Toby Sutherland, the police expert on marijuana, and his warning that we should not get too close to the bad guys.

He said, "We're not going to stop now. We'll just have to be careful. All stick together."

"All three of you?"

"Four. Derwent wants to come."

"You'll be easy to spot, that's for sure."

"But harder to rub out. Aren't we being melodramatic?"

"No. These guys don't play nice, I'm told."

"I hear you. Nicely."

"I'm talking dialect. Nice. But do you hear what I'm saying?"

"Joe, we're having a ball. Harold and Robert are arguing about what to wear. Robert says he's going to wear a fedora. He'd like to wear spats like George Raft but he can't find anyone who sells them."

"Is he going to carry a roscoe, too?"

"Don't be silly. Now listen, I'll be there tomorrow."

"What for?"

"I want to be in on it. Okay? Oh, by the way, the price of weed has doubled in the last twenty-four hours."

"Why?"

"Somebody's buying it all up. We keep hearing 'Russians.' Got a minute? Here's the story as we've put it together, what we've picked up on the street. Sometime soon the Russian mob is going to send a huge shipment of dope to Gdansk for onward shipment to St. Petersburg. They are presently gearing up for it by preparing to buy up all the weed on the market at one time, on a specific day. At that time they will be ready to pay twice the market price, up to five thousand dollars a pound, because they can get twice that or more in Russia. That's why there's a shortage right now — the dealers are hoarding, waiting for the word. The price didn't double immediately — it's not like gasoline, which doubles at the pump ten minutes after a refinery in Iran blows up. The pot dealers don't have agreements like the oil cartels and they want to keep their customers happy, so they may even take a slight loss in the short run — they are paying more for their supplies already. But the price is high now, and when the Russians have got their shipment together it will collapse, back to the old levels or less, so the dealers are nervous about getting stuck. Its just like the futures market in orange juice."

I said, "Why don't the Russians buy the pot as the dealers get it? Why wait for a specific date?"

"Holding on to pot is a risk. The more you are caught with, the longer the sentence, so everybody holds it for as short a time as possible. And don't forget the drug squad is under a cloud at the moment and they're looking for any brownie points they can earn. The Russians know that and they know that the squad will work actual overtime if necessary to catch them."

"When is this supposed to happen? The date the Russians will bring the money?"

"The word is, in the next few days. There's an air freight carrier that flies out of Frankfurt. This stuff will be crated up as herbal supplies, stimulants, you know — ground-up polar bears' balls and such. It's a well-established trade."

"What other routes are there?"

"Several. Detroit, but lately, the cross-border run has become tricky with all the security people at the U.S. customs looking for bombs. For them, everything looks like anthrax. Churchill. I didn't know there was an airport in Churchill."

"Manitoba? There's an airport there, all right." I said. "My father was in and out of Churchill just after the war, working for the railway. Churchill was part of the D.E.W. line. I didn't know it was still functioning. The Mounties police Manitoba, so all they have to do is tell their man in Churchill to keep his eyes open. But let me get the next move straight. At some point the Russians are going to drive around town picking up the pot these dealers are hoarding? When?"

"First the dealers are going to bring their stuff to one main dealer who will pay them for it. When it's all in one place, the Russians will pick it up. I told you the idea is to have it for as little time as possible before they pass it on. I imagine they've arranged to ship it out within hours of collecting it. Pearson airport sounds most likely."

"Do the Metro guys know all this? The drug squad?"

"We aren't really liaising with them, Joe."

I said, "I see. Don't go into any dark rooms, Timothy, and keep me in touch, won't you?"

Now I had one more call to make, to my father.

I found him at home, in Winnipeg; he was just finishing his supper. After the usual "how-are-you's" I said, "Dad, is the airport in Churchill still functioning?"

"As far as I know," he said. "I could find out. There's some kind of reunion up in Churchill every five years or so for former residents. I don't really qualify, but one time I took a trip up there on my own time, just to have a look around."

"Could you find out if there are any commercial planes flying out of Churchill? I could find out from the Internet, I guess, but maybe your pals would know more. Where else do they fly to from there besides Winnipeg? And you've given me another thought. Are there still ships using that port, other than grain boats? And where do they go to? And when does the last one in the season arrive and leave?"

"It's long gone for this year. The port's iced up already."

"So, again, Dad, could you find out if there's any little airline still flying up there, on skis, I guess, that kind of thing. There's no road in yet, is there?"

"No. I can ask around. So how's the missus?"

Three months before, well into Carole's second trimester, I had told him the news. He had been hoping for a grandchild for about twenty years, and regularly asked about the prospects. This time, to his "Not expecting, of course — no chance of that with you two," I had responded, "I've been meaning to call you."

"Jesus Christ," he said. "That sounds like good news. You're not just teasing me, are you?"

"No, but don't ask me or her again, okay, Dad? Not yet. We've become superstitious."

"That sounds good, too. Got your fingers crossed?"

"Yes."

"How about Carole?"

"She has, too"

"I bet you've thought about nothing else lately. It was a lot easier when we had you. Your mother and I got married, pulled the blinds down and the next day looked around for a good second-hand crib. We didn't hold the idea up to the light and analyze it to death."

Now he said, "I'll give Jenkins a call about Churchill and call you back. Don't go away. Then we can talk about your news."

"Dad ..."

But he'd hung up. That was always his way: give you a monologue then leave without saying goodbye, as if you've offended him. Maybe that's the Manitoba way.

ROGERO REPORTED THE NEXT DAY. "Three hundred," he said.

"You have three hundred friends and relatives cleaning here? I don't believe you." I'm generally a little dozy late in the day.

"Three hundred to fix the dint."

"Three hundred!"

"That's the best he can do. As a favour to me."

"You just saved me five hundred."

"It won't be ready for a couple of days."

"Tell him to take his time."

"He wants cash, you know, no cheques."

My introduction to the black economy. Cheers, I thought. "Tell him I'll give him a sack of used loonies, if he wants, guaranteed untraceable."

"Fifties are okay. Friday? Three days?"

"Here." I held out the car keys. "It's parked near the back fence."

"I'll get Romero to drive it. By the way, your guy is here again, sitting in his car."

I took a deep breath and ran down to the street and around the corner, and there he was, David Simmonds, dressed to kill, shaved head, granny glasses, earring and all.

Seeing him there, the chase over, I felt a little giddy. My first reaction was to run down to the car, fling open the door, and declaim, "David Simmonds, I believe!" but now I wanted to know what this was all about, and I didn't think he'd tell me. Besides, it was Timothy's case. I could help, though. I would cancel my class, stay close, follow him, see where he went.

But he was in a car, and Rogero had the keys to mine. I ran back to find Rogero, moving as fast as I could, but when I returned in the car Simmonds was gone.

I said to Rogero, "Did you notice anyone else, any other car?"

"There was a van delivering to the copy shop." He took a slip of paper from his pocket. "It said, 'All Your Stationery Needs' on the side. After that, nothing. You come back tomorrow."

"I will. Thanks, Rogero."

"Now I gotta go. Will I tell them to keep watching for him?"

"Yes, please. But I hope we'll find him first."

It was just as well. Simmonds would be bound to see me following him. Timothy arrived in my office, and I told him what had happened. "I can't follow him, anyway," I said. "He knows me."

"We'll take him on tomorrow night. Maybe he just goes home. Maybe the other side have rumbled him and taken him out"

"Who else do you read besides le Carré, Timothy? You need to work on your dialogue. I think 'rumbled' is English slang. Read some Elmore Leonard. He invented a new diction."

"See you tomorrow, Ace."

I went back to my office to find Mullins standing in the doorway.

"Coffee?" he asked. "How you doing with that instructor of yours who disappeared? Whatsisname, Simmonds?"

It was odd to see Herb was working late. He had carried from his hourly paid days a notion of a day's work for a day's pay that worked both ways; he didn't like to work overtime if he could help it. Apart from that, it was odd to see him away from his desk. In his own office he always stayed behind the counter, as it were. Now I noticed that he was wearing red running shoes with his business suit, like a news reader who only has to worry about what he looks like from the waist up. I looked at my watch. "Carole's expecting me home. Let me call her, then I'll fill you in. Don't you have to get home?"

"It can wait. Bring me up to date."

In the cafeteria, I told him the story so far, including the fact that Simmonds had been seen and the plan to follow him the next evening.

Herb said, "That's real cute. Yeah. I wouldn't get too close, though. This guy sounds weird. Now, let me ask you a question. What's the difference between 'Scots,' 'Scottish,' and 'Scotch'?"

It was some time before I realized that Herb was not working late to improve his knowledge of the language; he was keeping an eye on me. It was one of those realizations that came all at once, in a blinding flash, as they say, like my realization that Toft was the author of the letters, a discovery that came when I was trying to figure out something else.

And then I got a pleasant surprise. Crossing the street on the way to the subway I saw two students I recognized, pausing on either side of a car parked at a meter. As I slowed down, willing them to get in and drive away before I had to say hello, I realized that the car they were leaning on was a new Peugeot wagon, surely an odd match for those two. Simultaneously, I wondered what they were doing around the college on this night because I thought mine was their only class and tonight was not a class night. Then I watched the one who was working on the door fail to open it and reorganize himself for another assault on the lock.

Then I realized what I was seeing.

As I reached him, the character trying the door was leaning nonchalantly against the car, and only looked up when I paused. It was a delicious moment.

"Evening, fellas," I said. "What's up?"

The one by the door — Slapshot One — recovered first. "We was just having a smoke before class," he said.

"Yeah," said Slapshot Two.

"What class would that be?" I asked.

"French," Slapshot One said, after a few seconds.

"Yeah," said the other.

I burst out laughing, and Slapshot One grinned slyly. No one was being fooled.

I cut to the chase. "You know whose car this is?"

"Yeah. Guy teaches Economics. He's in class until nine o'clock."

"How do you know?"

Slapshot One got a look of tired irritation on his face. "What does it matter?" the expression said.

Right. What did it matter? All they needed was a calendar to know who was teaching when, and to watch the lot and the adjacent street for a few days to see who drove what car. It was a perfect set-up for two fake students.

I said, "How many so far?"

Slapshot One said, "You ain't thinking of going to the cops? Jesus, he's on probation already." He pointed at his mate. "They'll have him inside, sure."

Slapshot Two said, "We got something to trade. Tell him about the teacher, Robbo."

"What teacher?" I asked.

"The teacher who fucked off. We seen him."

"Where?"

"Around here. Wanna trade?"

"We already know about him. You got anything else to trade? Tell me something I don't know."

"He's a cop," Robbo said.

As soon as Robbo said it, I felt as if a button had been pressed on one of those Paris Metro maps, linking up the whole route.

Robbo said, "We knew first day when he walked into class. You can always tell, even with an asshole like that, even now when he's in that fuckin' stoopid disguise. He was hangin' around here tonight.

He's on a stakeout."

"You think he might have seen you?"

"So what? We're stoodents, having a smoke." He grinned and held up a battered briefcase. I wondered whose it was.

Robbo said, "He's the one to worry about us, right?"

"Okay, we trade that one. Now, another one." And I asked them about the stolen Subaru.

"What night was that?"

I counted back the days and told him. A huge gummy grin broke out on his face. "We was in Lakehead," he said. "For a tournament. We was there for three days. We just heard someone had took the Subaru when we got back."

That would do. It was probably true. Hearing about the Subaru had given them the idea, but they hadn't had time to do anything about it yet. "Good," I said. "But if another car disappears, I'll turn you in. Now fuck off."

So, a cop. But what kind of cop? Not one of Metro's finest; I trusted the word of my former student in headquarters. The Mounties? The combination of drugs and Russians would interest them, surely. But why was Simmonds watching the copy shop?

Dinner — call it supper, now — was toasted bacon and tomato sandwiches, followed by three of those Portuguese custard tarts. Not bad, but not like it had been lately.

I figured Carole must be close to term, but she had warned me not to keep asking.

CHAPTER TWENTY-TWO

THE EXTENSION CLASSES STARTED AT six and I had filled in the time between the end of the day classes and the beginning of evening classes by reading some pamphlets Carole had collected from her prenatal clinic. I wondered how much of the information was medical and how much simply opinion. Breastfeeding, for instance is back in fashion, but circumcision is no longer favoured, at least in this pamphlet. Bonding is another activity undergoing a rethink: the writer of this pamphlet is sure that a child bonds with its parent for life by the time it is four months old. But what if this kind of advice — I thought of it as behavioural advice based on guesswork and theory — turned out to have guessed wrong? What if all the responses including love and hate can be managed electrically by shoving needles into the newborn's hippothermus, or whatever that thing's called.

Timothy stuck his head around the door. He'd been churning with excitement about "the case" as he called it and wanting to talk about it more or less continually. Now he had been watching the street for Simmonds since four o'clock.

"He never came," he said. "I waited for hours. Now, I want to show you this. Interesting." He drew a little bundle of photographs from his pocket and passed one across the desk. It was a picture of Simmonds, granny glasses, earring in place, standing on a curb.

"Where did this come from?"

"Harry. One of my people," Timothy said grandly. "You met him. Ginger hair, gap-toothed. He saw your man yesterday in the neighbourhood, on Wellesley, actually, and tried to follow him, but he got away, Simmonds or Tosti, I mean. But my man had a loaded camera around his neck, pretending to be a tourist, and he got this picture."

"That was lucky. Seeing him, recognizing him, and having a camera, I mean."

"I told you, Harry always has his camera with him. He's become one of those people who take pictures of everything. Invite him to dinner and he's standing on the doorstep, taking your picture as you open the door. You have to take it away from him or he keeps it up all through dinner. He's like Harpo Marx except with a flash camera instead of a motor horn. "'Flash,' he goes, when he wants to say something. 'Flash, flash.'"

"So, he's still around." I looked at the picture more carefully. "And so is *he*," I said. "Well, well."

Timothy looked over my shoulder. I pointed to the other figure standing outside a fruit stand, fingering an apple. He was about twenty yards beyond Simmonds.

"You know that guy?"

"Indeed I do. His name is Sargent, and he is a policeman in plain clothes. See? Constable Sargent." I looked again to make sure. "But I heard from someone else last night that Simmonds is a cop, too. So what's going on? They must be up to something clever. The first time he came to my office Sargent told me he was looking for Simmonds. He's found him now, hasn't he? They don't look like the best of friends, though, do they? So what are they up to?"

"You'll have to find him first."

"I think I know how to do that."

The reason why Simmonds had not shown up in his car to wait at the same spot had just jumped out at me. Herb Mullins. He was working late that night. He had warned Simmonds. It had to be. I wanted to run down the corridor and shout obscenities at Herb Mullins there and then but I got a better idea, one that would get rid of any doubts. I strolled down to Herb's office, taking my time.

Herb was in his office, and I told him the latest development. "What next?" he asked.

"My boys are going to look for Simmonds downtown," I said.

"Forget about staking out the copy shop?"

"There's no point, now, is there? He's been tipped off about us."

"You think?" He waited for more, then said, "Maybe he's got an accomplice."

I almost laughed, and I'd have jumped on Herb right there, but I had Simmonds hooked now and I didn't want to create a chance for Herb to warn him.

THE NEXT DAY I TAUGHT "A Slumber Did My Spirit Seal" while I was waiting for zero hour. Over the years I have lovingly polished a presentation that consists entirely of questions, easy ones. Step by step the class unlocks secrets in every line, out of the dreamlike language of the first stanza and the scientific vocabulary of the second they ease themselves into the allegory until they feel the full impact of the "rocks and stones and trees" of the last line. I wished Ron Crabtree had been there, because for once I might have taught him something.

One bright girl said, "But this is obviously an epitaph, carved on her gravestone, and I thought Wordsworth loved Nature. Isn't Lucy some kind of symbol of Nature? But she dies." And we were off, moving satisfyingly into the question of where, in the poem, Lucy dies. We spent the hour and could have used another half hour, but the mood created would not easily be recovered the next day, so I left it there.

Afterwards, on my way back to my room, I realized that I had probably talked about Lucy for the last time.

SIMMONDS TURNED UP JUST AFTER four in a different car, and parked a block away from the college. He opened a book, took off his glasses, and started to read. I watched him from a second-floor window of the Television Arts department on the other side of the building. I waited until he looked settled, then made my way down to the street level and opened the passenger door and climbed in. Simmonds' face when he saw who was sitting next to him reminded me of Buster Keaton's when he was trying to sort out his music in *Limelight*.

"Did Herb tell you we wouldn't be watching tonight?" I asked.

It took a long time, but finally he saw that I had to know what was going on. "You know about Herb Mullins?" he asked.

"I do now. He's been in on this from the start, right? Recommended you be hired so you had a good cover." And then some of the rest fell into place. "And Tommy Stokoe, the security guard? Both of them recruited to put you in place as an undercover cop. Right? How about the president? And my department chairman?"

"Not them, no. Just the first two. And Herb Mullins didn't tell me you wouldn't be watching. I just parked far enough away so you wouldn't see me."

Probably still lying, I thought. Still. I said, "Not quite far enough, apparently. Let's get some coffee and you can tell me what else I don't know. Okay?"

He didn't move. I said. "Let's have a chat, okay?" I was nearly shouting. "If you want to keep this fucking thing quiet, that is." I had no idea what "this" was, but it worked.

In the cafeteria, coffee in front of us, Simmonds waited for me to ask questions.

I said. "First, why the fancy dress? Playing some kind of game, are you?"

"I had to go underground. I saw a dealer from Edmonton who knew me as a member of the squad there. If he saw me I knew he'd spread the word, or worse. These guys play for high stakes."

I let it go, even though I suspected that Simmonds was trying to impress me with the seriousness of his world. The silly disguise spoke of someone who enjoyed acting. I said, "Okay, what is Constable Sargent up to? You know he's watching you, don't you?"

He sucked at a tooth thoughtfully. I'd scored a hit. "No, I didn't know that."

"From day one. I have a picture of him watching you on Wellesley two days ago."

Simmonds spelled it out slowly, repeating what I had said. "You have a picture of me and Sargent. Christ!" He shifted in his seat, banging against the table and sending the dregs of someone's coffee to the floor. "Okay, here's the whole thing. See, the drug squad here has been under investigation, and when I had to go undercover to avoid the dealer from Edmonton, I figured that I might as well go the whole way and disappear. See, as long as the squad knew who I was, and what I was doing, if there was still one bad apple in the squad, then all the dealers would know, too. I figured I might learn something on my own that I could tell them when I was ready. So then I guess they sent Sargent to find me and see what I was doing."

"He'd already found you is my point. He was following you around."

"Maybe he figured I had made some progress, so he was keeping tabs."

"Jesus Christ. Did you? Did you make any progress they don't know about? Don't get coy. You owe me something."

Simmonds experienced the usual struggle of someone in the know, the struggle between wanting to keep it to himself and wanting to show off how much he knew.

I said, "To save you time, I know all about the Russian scheme. Maybe you don't know?"

He smiled like a man with a full house, waiting to be called. I felt a little sorry for him then. From where I sat it looked as if the guys on the drug squad knew everything that he knew, and maybe a little more. Simmonds, I thought, had become a little giddy, so pleased with himself that he didn't consider that the Metro police weren't just sitting there, keeping their thumbs warm, wondering what was happening.

But I wasn't sure Simmonds had told me the whole truth yet. I said, "He was from Edmonton, this guy who would recognize you?"

"Right. I arrested him once out there."

"So what if he had seen you?"

"He would have warned everybody else about me. All the dealers."

"So you disappeared."

"It was the only way. And I couldn't let you know because, well, I couldn't trust you to stay quiet, especially now you needed another teacher."

"I understand how it was from your point of view. Someday try to understand mine and don't ask me for a reference. Okay?"

I thought of something else. I said, "So you weren't targeting the gay district?"

Simmonds said, "The squad had given me a few dealers they knew about. Some of them were in the area where they had booked me a room in the hotel —"

"The Jubilee?"

"Right. It used to be a home for a big dealer, but someone bought it and they are trying to make a go of it as a regular tourist hotel. It seemed like a good place to watch the district from. I think it was just the crummiest hotel they could find. See, it wasn't their idea to parachute me in from Edmonton and I think maybe I pissed them off."

"Now, tell me what you are doing around here, tonight."

"The college is on the list the squad gave me. They think someone has been using the copy shop to deal dope to the students. So that's what I'm doing. Watching. Oh, shit. Here they come."

I looked around to follow his gaze. From the far end of the cafeteria, Constable Sargent was advancing on us. Simmonds looked away, seeming to hunch slightly, waiting for the blow.

When he reached our table, Sargent said, "Mind if I join you?" in the flat voice of someone looking for a seat, but with the slight edge that made the words fighting talk.

"Who told you we were here?" I asked.

"The cleaner in your office. He said, 'Mr. Barley is in the cafeteria with the guy in the car.' Just like that. We didn't have to torture him or anything." He looked at Simmonds. "I figured that must be you. So tell me who you were waiting for and then fuck off. Okay?"

Simmonds thought about that for a few seconds, then shrugged. "There's a white panel truck that's been rented three times from the same agency down on Front Street. They rent it for the day, then take it back at night. They took it out the day before yesterday, this time, for a week. I was planning to follow it. You can take over now."

"I'll tell them to watch it round the clock until tomorrow night," Sargent said.

I said, "Why are you talking about tomorrow night? Didn't somebody say their operation is the night after?"

"It's very elementary," Sargent said. "The word is that the day after tomorrow is the big night, but we've also found out that they are really going in tomorrow. See, we are supposed to think that Saturday is the big day; so we are supposed to relax for a day as we get ready to catch them. But by then they've long gone."

"So, will you pounce tomorrow? Is that what you're saying?"

"I don't know about 'pounce.' We don't know how they'll work it yet. All we know is that tomorrow, we hope, the Russians are set to buy the dope and ship it back to Russia. Probably they'll fly it to Frankfurt. We've already got all the dogs and handlers doing double shift down at Pearson Airport. If we lose them here they won't get through the airport. They'll probably move in the middle of the evening when there are plenty of people about. Now I want some more coffee." He walked to the counter.

Alone with Simmonds I said, "Okay, what's going on?"

Simmonds' face was blank, but smugly, deceitfully blank. "How do you mean?"

"You know fucking well how I mean. Why are you looking so goddamn pleased with yourself?"

Finally, after about a minute of making up his mind, he said, "Joe, I have to tell you, what you just heard is the story everybody's supposed to believe, put together for your benefit by the so-called Russians."

"The so-called Russians?"

Simmonds looked around to locate Sargent, who was now paying for his coffee. He said, "I've been hearing about the Russians from the start, but a couple of days ago it occurred to yours truly that I hadn't heard or overheard a word of Russian. So I started asking around. No one else has, either. That doesn't bother anyone else, apparently, but it bothered me. But there aren't any Russians."

"Jesus Christ! Then who is concocting this scheme?"

Before he could answer, Sargent returned to the table. "Someone's wigwagging us," he said. "You know him?"

It was Timothy. He came through the cafeteria at a trot, waving his cellphone. (Later I found I had inadvertently switched mine off.) "It's Carole," he said, when he reached us, gasping for breath. "She's been taken to hospital. Perhaps she's having a miscarriage."

Sargent said, "Who's Carole?"

I said, "My wife."

Sargent said, "I'll take us down. Which hospital?" He started to order a car on his cellphone.

I started to calm them down, to tell them my wife was having a baby, not a miscarriage, then I thought, why not? It'll be quicker, so I looked serious, and stood up. "The Women's College. The maternity wing."

Timothy said, "The General, Joe. She said not the Women's College, the General. The General. The emergency department. Joe, there's something wrong."

"Let's go," Sargent said. "But not you," to Timothy, who was preparing to join us.

Timothy said, "Joe?" He was distraught.

I said, to Sargent, "He's family. I need him."

"Okay," Sargent said. Then, to Simmonds, "But there's no room for you, buddy."

ANOTHER REASON TO GO WITH the flow was that I've always wanted to do an emergency vehicle run, in a police car for choice, racing down Avenue Road, screaming around Upper Canada College, through all the red lights, around Queen's Park on two wheels, coming to a juddering halt at the hospital steps. But now we were doing it, all I could think was, "*Could we go a bit faster? Just in case.*"

Another thing: I teach *A Farewell to Arms* whenever I get a chance, and not too long ago I was involved in the recovery of a previously unknown Hemingway manuscript, so you might say that I'm soaked in the old soak's prose. That's my only excuse for not being able to get the words from the end of the novel out of my mind: "What if she should die. People don't die. But what if she should die? Etc., Etc. How about that, what if she should die?"

Why couldn't I have my own words? Is that what teaching English does to you? Fills you up with second-hand language, and the emotions to go with them?

We pulled up to the emergency entrance of the Toronto General and I ran through the doors looking for a reception desk. A clerk looked up. "Carole," I said. "Carole Trainor. She just came in."

"Take a seat over there."

"What's the matter with her? Where is she?"

A nurse came through the inner doors. I grabbed her arm.

"Carole Trainor," I said. "What happened?"

"I've just been seeing to her. She's in the first corridor on the right."

"Is she okay?"

"She's in a hospital, isn't she? No, she'll be all right soon. We're keeping her in tonight and transferring her tomorrow to Women's College, where she belongs." She took my arm, and looked around to see if anyone was watching. "You the father? The baby's father, I mean, not hers. Here, go through this door, down to the far end and turn right. We haven't got a bed for her yet."

I scampered past the row of patients lined up on trolleys along the wall of the corridor until I came to her, lying with her eyes closed, on the first trolley around the corner. I said, in as ordinary a voice as I could manage, "Carole?"

She opened her eyes, made a rueful face, and started to cry.

This wasn't in the cards. I think I've only ever seen her tears once before. I said, "The nurse said it was all right. Why are you here, not the maternity hospital? Why are you crying?"

She said, "The cab driver was scared I'd have the baby in his cab. Hold on to me."

Now I was totally at sea. Her words were a signal, but of what? Sadness? Joy? Hello? A need for comfort?

I said, holding tight (or tightly) and kissing her gently, near tears myself, "What's the matter?"

"Have you seen him?"

"Who?"

"Him, him. They took him away to wash him. He's got a red face and ginger hair. Make them show you."

"You're still crying."

"I was frightened. In the end it was all so quick."

"But it's all right now?"

"Yes. Hold on to me."

"I'll do better than that." I was sort of half sitting on the stretcher. I slid down on to my knees, and kissed her face. "Marry me," I said. I was crying too, now, just a little.

She gave a little shriek, then, to cover it, said, "I thought you'd never ask."

The old man on the next trolley along the wall sat up to watch us, looking pleased.

I said, "I have to get a job. We need somewhere bigger to live, with room for a cot. And we need to do it all soon, now we've had a blessing on our endeavours," giving her Mirabel's line from her favourite play, an old joke between us.

"Odious endeavours," she said, giving me back Millament's line, grinning a bit, finally.

I said, "See? We have a lot in common."

The nurse rounding the corner said, "We are taking her into her room now. If you wait down the hall I'll tell her when she's ready to see you."

Carole put out her hand to touch me. "Go home," she said. "I'm tired. Come and get me tomorrow."

I said, "Timothy wanted to see you. He's outside."

"I'm too tired now. Tell him we want him to be godfather."

WHEN THE NURSE CAME BACK she was carrying an envelope of blanket. "Look," she said. "See?" She opened the blanket and showed me. Carole was right: red face, ginger hair. I said, "Can I hold him?"

She put him in my arms and I wet my finger and touched the tip of his nose to mark him as mine, and handed him back.

CHAPTER TWENTY-THREE

SIMMONDS AND THE POLICE CAR had gone. Timothy sprang up, "Is she all right?" He was very angry. "You never came out," he said. "Why didn't you come out?"

I took his arm and led him outside, gave him the good news, and explained why she was staying the night in the General and then moving over to the Women's College as he threw his arms around me in an enormous hug. I told him how Carole wanted him to be godfather.

"Me?" he said. "Me?" He was electrified. "What are you going to call him? I want to practise his name."

I took Timothy home and went back to our apartment, unable to stop thinking of how I would be now if I had had the bad news that Lieutenant Henry got.

I called Carole's sister, and she started to shout at me for not telling her sooner, so I hung up. I didn't have to call anyone else, then I remembered my father and knew I had to call him, tell him we weren't interested in Churchill anymore, and bring him up to date on his grandson. He started to talk before I could tell him anything.

"Here's what else I've found," he said. "While I can still read what I took down. First of all, the season's been expanded a bit. It now goes to the end of October, and they reckon with this global warming it might go into November, though the ice floes might be dangerous. That's it." He paused. "Is she still working?"

"What? Who?"

"How many women you been trying to put in the club lately? Carole, of course. She's not strong, you know. Now she's got a bun in the oven, she needs looking after, at her age, if I'm ever to become a grandfather."

"She can still lift herself out of her chair."

"You should move out of that place you live in. Get yourself a proper apartment. You got enough money?"

The fact that he was probably right, that we had been thinking the same thing, was irrelevant. I said, "This is a proper apartment. We don't share it with anybody."

"It's part of a house. You need something with elevators, soundproof, so she can get a good night's sleep."

"I'll let you know what Carole thinks." I took a breath, getting ready with the big news. "In the meantime, thanks for the help."

But he had hung up already. I had some thinking to do, and I poured myself a Kronenberg, my new favourite, took out a pad of lined paper, and wrote at the top, "The First Day of My New Life." I knew I was playing about, making up a bit of writing for Carole to come across by accident, but I started anyway.

1) Get a permanent job.
2) Look for a bigger apartment.
3) Newer, safer car?
4) Buy a crib.
5) Really tell my father.

That looked like everything and I made sure the place was tidy in case Carole should sign herself out of the hospital in the night and bring the infant phenomenon home before I woke up. There was no chance of that, of course. I was performing a ritual for my own absolution, making sure I'd done all I could. And now, just in case somehow he got the news by some other route before I told him, I called my father back. "Dad," I said. "I forgot to ask. What's your first name?"

"Joseph, of course, same as yours. Actually it's not. It's Josiah. Josiah Matthew. I don't tell everybody. Why?"

"Carole will like that."

"What's that got to do with anything? What? Why? Hey. You trying to tell me something? When?"

"Today, Dad. You hung up before I could tell you. You always do that."

"You're not joking? I'll kill you, you little bastard. Right, I'm on my way. I'll be there on Friday. Hang on: you can't call a little kid Josiah, can you? These days."

"Carole can."

"Yeah, sure, I guess she can. We can call him Joe at home. Or Jos. No, Joe. I'll see you on Friday. No need to meet me. Give her my love, and kiss little Joe for me."

You could practically hear him grinning.

I spent the next day holding Carole's hand for as long as they would let me before they sent me away.

TIMOTHY PHONED BEFORE I GOT to bed. He was in the rotunda at police headquarters. I told him what my father had said, including the information about Churchill just in case it might still have some relevance. I was very tired.

Timothy said, "That's luck isn't it? You call your father a thousand miles away and he knows just the man to speak to in Churchill, six hundred miles north of him."

"It's not that strange. I grew up in Winnipeg. Everybody in Winnipeg knows someone in Churchill. Churchill is populated by emigrants from Winnipeg. It was never settled in the sense that towns like Brandon and Dauphin and The Pas were settled a hundred years ago by people getting off a train and making a mark in the soil and claiming the land for a quarter mile around."

"That's very interesting, Joe. And what else did you did you learn today, apart from your father's Churchill story?" He was bubbling, obviously sitting on news he was dying to be asked about.

I said, "I think I learned that a gang of crooks, pretending to be Russians, will very soon be assembling a truckload of marijuana, but I don't know what they plan to do from there."

"Well done, Joe. Now I'll tell you the rest." He was spluttering with excitement. "Can you come here for an hour? It's showtime."

Why not? Joe, Jos, Joshua, Josh? I wouldn't sleep anyway. I put on some clothes and drove down to College Street.

TIMOTHY SAID, "WHILE WE WERE waiting for you at the hospital, Constable Sargent and I got quite chummy. I told him about wanting to write a detective novel, and he said I should stay in touch and he would tell me anything I needed to know — technical details, that sort of thing. Actually, I think he wants to write one himself — he was asking me about agents and so on — so we can trade. I'll be like Holden Caulfield's roommate — I'll stick in a few commas for him. Anyway, he said he'd call me and sure enough, he did, tonight, telling me to get a cab up to headquarters right away; they were planning a stakeout. I think his colleague was a bit pissed off at having me in the back seat but Sargent outranked him, so away we went. It was all quite simple, really. We drove to this house on Maitland, you know, off Church south of college, actually we drove past it and went around the block. On the way, Sargent pointed out the four other police cars that were parked, waiting. And then we parked, too, to wait, while Sargent filled me full of police lore — that's l-o-r-e. Even his partner thawed a bit and added his two cents' worth to some of Sargent's examples. It was fascinating. I was scribbling in my little notebook like a madman.

"Then it happened. The white van drew up, three characters got out and ran into the house, one of them carrying a sack; Sargent said something into his walkie-talkie or whatever they have and plainclothes police appeared and swarmed around the house and disappeared inside. In no time a couple of them reappeared with the three characters in handcuffs, leaving the other police, I would think, to search the house. I've still got a lot of questions to ask, because Sargent's partner told me to stay quiet. Then we came back here, and now we're waiting again. Here we go."

Sargent said, "Hi there, Tim. There's just the copy-shop people to come. You can sit down on the floor against the wall if you want," he said to three men in handcuffs.

I said, "'Tim' now, is it?"

Two more men, manacled together, came through the door, accompanied by two uniformed policemen. Another plainclothes man with them appeared and called Sargent to one side and the two retreated to the glass-walled enclosure in the centre of the rotunda where they got into an intense conversation. Through the glass we saw Sargent pick up an internal phone and speak to someone. He put his head through the door. "Where's the van?" he asked of the room.

"Right outside," a young policeman answered. "I drove it back myself. Impound it for evidence?"

"Go get the money out of it. Bring it in here. All of it."

"I already did that," another officer said. "The swag. It's in the trunk of our car."

"Go get it."

When the officer returned he was holding a gunny sack which really looked as if it ought to have the word SWAG stencilled on it. The man Sargent had probably spoken to on the phone now appeared, and the three of them huddled around the desk, looking at the contents of the sack

"Right," Sargent said. "Officer Dacre and I will deal with these three" — he indicated the three handcuffed men — the "Russians" — "and these two from the copy shop." The "Russians" stayed silent and close to each other. The two men from the copy shop were led away to be charged. One of them, more relaxed than his friend, was teasing the other man. "Oh, yes," he was saying. "They use a glove, but they really rootle around in there to make sure you haven't hidden anything." "No way," his partner was protesting, with passion. "Not me. I'll get my lawyer." The teaser shook his head vigorously. "The lawyer can't stop them. It's like a breath test. There's nothing to it. You just bend over." The two of them shuffled into line, the victim still in noisy denial.

Sargent led the prisoners, signalling Timothy and me to follow, into an inner office where we sat down while the policeman listed the charges.

"First," he said, "there's dealing in an illegal substance. Then there's trying to evade arrest. That's the other two," he pointed at the copy-shop pair. "As for you three, there's trading in drugs at the wholesale level, whatever the law calls it. You certainly grow it, too, and in a minute we'll get you to tell us where and how. Then, when we search that van and the print shop in the basement of the copy shop, I imagine we'll find all kinds of documents — forgeries, no doubt —

passports, Landed Immigrant cards, stuff like that, and we'll nail you for illegal entry. There'll be enough to hold you for about twenty years or put you on the next Aeroflot."

"You're a clever man, officer, but you'll not be sending us to Russia," one of the trio said. "That was just a blind, d'ye see? I'm legally landed, well enough, and so are my friends."

One of the other two said, "Declan, tell them to call the embassy." An educated voice, but not Canadian or English.

Timothy confirmed it, like an extra in a play finally justifying his presence on stage. "It's the Irish mob," he said. "Glory be to God. But there's no snot. Where's the snot?"

I thought the gang's spokesman, who was pretty well-dressed by any standards — they all were — might kill him, but he just said, "I don't keep a pig in the kitchen, either. Can we get on?"

Timothy's voice reminded Sargent of the presence of the non-combatants. "All right, you guys," he said. He moved his finger to describe a circle over our two heads. "Thanks for the help. Tim, we'll get together later, whenever you want, eh?"

Sargent waited until we had moved through the door, then started barking orders.

As we left, Simmonds was sitting in the little glass-enclosed office in the rotunda, talking to the duty sergeant. I tapped on the glass, gave him a thumbs-up, mouthing, "You were right!"

He nodded and spread his hands, banging into the desk sergeant's telephone. I think he was trying for a gesture of modesty.

CHAPTER TWENTY-FOUR

IN THE COFFEE SHOP AT the corner of Yonge Street, Timothy ordered drinks. He said "It was all a con, then, by three Irishmen, looking for easy pickings in the colonies. Do you feel a letdown?"

I said, "Simmonds had warned me to expect a surprise. He guessed there were no Russians."

"Did he, indeed? Clever fellow. I'll try and have a chat with him. Where are you off to now?"

"See Carole, then home."

"Can I come?"

Taken aback, I said, "It's ten o'clock!"

He said, "Let's take her some flowers, and a new book, just in case."

"Why?"

"Because I don't want to go home, my home." He was very down-in-the-mouth. The party was over. But he seemed to be suffering something more than a letdown after the excitement.

"Derwent?" I guessed. "He still not speaking?"

"No. Yes. He's still not speaking."

I said, blundering casually into no man's land, "Maybe your relationship is over."

He leaned back to get me in his sights. "No more glib remarks like that, Joseph, if you please. What do you know about our relationship?"

I started to speak but he carried on. "Nothing. Do you? I'll give you an insight. In England married couples can get a divorce these days when a relationship is suffering what they call "irretrievable marital breakdown." That's where Derwent and I are at. Okay?"

"I'm sorry."

"For what?" he asked.

Fuck this, I thought. A thoughtless remark, maybe, but not a criminal act. "For you in your present misery; for me for having to pay for being glib; and for Derwent too, while we're at it."

"For Derwent, too," he repeated. "Yes, let's not forget Derwent." He leaned forward, rejoining me. "Carole would have been a blessed relief for an hour." He smiled a little, I thought forgivingly.

There was a call waiting for me at home from my father, but I decided it could wait. I didn't want to talk to him any more about Carole, yet.

CAROLE, SITTING UP IN HER hospital bed, laughed. A night on Diazepam or whatever had done the trick. "Tell me again," she said. "Simmonds smelled something funny from the start, about the copy shop, I mean, but he sat on it until he figured it out?"

"He wanted to track it back to the source, the greenhouse where they were growing the stuff. He thought that the van was involved in the delivery. He never got to the source, though, because there was no source. The Irish Russians were just selling here what they bought somewhere else, probably in Vancouver, cheap."

"The Russians." Carole laughed some more. "The Dublin mob, glory be to God."

"They worked a long time to set it up, sending out the gossip on the grapevine, turning the whole gay district into a Dublin pub, all rumours and gossip about the Russians."

Carole said, "There's still more to come, though. So far you've got three Irishmen imitating a Russian gang, just to buy and sell an extra large batch of dope. I would have thought there are easier ways."

I said, "Criminals are not necessarily clever, even the educated ones. I read that somewhere. And these are Irish criminals, remember."

"What does that mean?"

"They're suspicious of everybody. It makes it hard for them to think straight."

Carole said, "If they weren't going to get twice the going rate by shipping it to Russia, what were they really up to? I mean now all they would have got is a very big sack of dope for which they paid more, maybe, than they would get from selling it. It doesn't make sense."

I said, "We'll have to wait for the ending. Did you know Timothy is planning to write a novel, a detective story, about a gay Toronto cop? He says there are none in Toronto — novels about gay cops, he means."

Carole giggled. "I can't wait," she said. "Tell him to dedicate it to Josiah. Ask him to come and see me. I'll cheer him up."

It made sense finally only when Sargent went to deposit the loot in the police safe and was told by the sergeant in charge of the safe what he really had. Two days later, Sargent asked me to come into his office, and from there he took me to Fran's for coffee where he told me what I would read about in the paper the next day. I agreed to keep some part of the story between us, him and me. Not even Timothy would know the whole truth, because you can't trust civilians not to tell someone else.

THE NEXT DAY THE *Toronto Star* had the story. The headlines — big, confident — announced, POLICE SET TRAP FOR FORGERS.

The story told of how the police had spent some months patiently unpicking a scheme by an Irish gang to unload hundreds of thousands of dollars in forged American notes in payment for a huge quantity of marijuana. Getting wind of the scheme, and needing an undercover operator who was completely unknown to the dealers, the police had borrowed a specialist from the Edmonton force who had been able to put the scheme together and help to plan the response, a brilliant and successful sting.

This undercover agent tracked the nerve centre of the operation to an address on Maitland Street, and then watched the house until, as he put it, "the rats emerged." Through another source that the police are not willing to identify, the police were able to find out the actual time and date of the operation, and put together a coordinated plan to net the criminals in the act of trying to swindle the dealers.

For part of the time while he was undercover, Sergeant Simmonds passed as a teacher of Business Correspondence at Hambleton College. Mr. Joseph Barley, in charge of non-credit courses in the extension arm of the English department at Hambleton College, said, "He was a thoroughly qualified instructor in the subject, and had he continued would no doubt have taught the whole course satisfactorily. There have been no complaints from the students about Mr. Simmonds or his replacement."

SIMMONDS CALLED THE NEXT MORNING to say goodbye. "I enjoyed working with you, Joe. The teaching, I mean," he said.

I felt slightly shamed, but not much. We had agreed the night before that he would not be looking for his job back. I remember how I had wanted to deliver a ranting lecture about the sacred duty of a teacher, about the sacrifices people made to attend night school, all that stuff. But I also remembered what a wise old foreman on a construction crew had told me once: that you don't give a man shit and fire him, too. One or the other.

I said, "Good luck, David. But tell me, before you go, how come they gave you so much credit? The last I heard was of them leaving you out of the action entirely."

"Yeah, they were pissed off at having to look for me when I went under. But when they came to putting together the story for the press, they couldn't leave me out — too many people knew about me by then, including you. And I needed something good to take back to Edmonton. And we still had the dealer who nobody knows is an informer, and Sargent wanted to keep him under wraps. So we put our heads together and came up with the story you read. It works, doesn't it? I thought it sounded good."

"Timothy clipped it for his notebook. He says to say goodbye, by the way."

"Tell all your gay friends goodbye from me." Something crashed at his end. After a pause, Simmonds said, "Sorry, I dropped the phone. See you." He hung up.

"BLUEBELL ISN'T COMPLAINING," JACK CHEVAL said when I saw him on Monday morning. "It doesn't reflect badly on the college, and he likes the publicity. He offered to go on television to give a statement himself, but none of the stations were interested."

"Is he pleased enough to give me a job?"

"I'm glad you've raised that, Joe. I've just finished talking to the Business department. They've been getting a lot of calls from students wanting to take your course, the one that the policeman taught. Sawchuk, their deputy chairman, wants to take it over. He feels the college shouldn't have courses that are not supervised by qualified academic staff, in this case he means people with what he calls experience in the business world. The only experience he's had is of bankrupting his family's dry cleaning business, but that's beside the point, I guess."

"He wants us to drop it?"

"He wants to take it over, I said. And he can. That means we are going to be hard put next year to find enough work for even the regular faculty."

"Are there any daytime hours left?"

"A couple of the tenured people are already being put on special assignment in the library because there isn't enough work to go around."

"So, are you trying to tell me I'm to be laid off, or whatever the term is?"

"I think three hours at night are safe. You can count on that."

"I can count on getting a third of a regular workload for a ninth of the minimum pay, you mean? I can't live on that."

"It'll only be for a year, I would hope. I've got three people going on sabbatical the year after, and under the terms of the sessional faculty agreement, you would have priority for any work that is left over."

"All I have to do is find some honest work to support myself for a year, then I might get back in, part-time?"

"Have you done anything about getting your degree?"

"I've got my degree. It's called Master of Arts. I wrote a thesis and everything. My dad is very proud of me."

"We don't even interview M.A.'s anymore. You know that."

"Maybe I could teach Remedial English. Would I need special qualifications for that?"

"Yes."

"Jack, I've been teaching here for twice as long as you. I can supply you with copies of my student evaluations. I am universally liked by my colleagues, except Love who is a prick and doesn't like you, either. And my wife just had a baby, remember."

"You'll need to look for something permanent, then."

WHEN I CALLED ON ATKINSON I knew that he too knew all about Simmonds from the beginning. I understood why he had had to keep the knowledge secret. But where did he get the idea of palming Simmonds off on me in the first place?

He said, "You know, Joe, I rely on getting along with the Metro Police. They do me a lot of favours, and they came to me because they knew about you, and figured I could get you to find a spot for him. I said no, but then a few days later I got talking to Herb Mullins at a farewell party for the canteen manager and he told me you needed someone real fast, so it seemed like a nice fit without me having to get into the act."

I stood up. "I also came to tell you that come April I'm going to be looking for regular full-time employment so I won't be able to moonlight for you. Not that there's been much work lately."

"How about working for me full-time?"

"You mean salary, benefits, pension, all that?"

"Oh, no. Everybody here except me is on per diem."

"And how has everyone done this year?"

"Most of them get three or four days a week, except around Christmas. Of course, most of them are former cops on pension, like me, so they don't need a lot of money. "

"Thanks for your trust, Bill, but I have responsibilities. Maybe I can use you as a reference?"

CHAPTER TWENTY-FIVE

HERB MULLINS SAID, "STOP LOOKING for a fight, Joe. I admit it was my idea, mine and Atkinson's. But there was a little pressure from upstairs, too."

"Who?"

"Numbnuts. Bluebell. I wouldn't do it just for the cops, but then they asked Bluebell, who's on one of their committees — Community Relations, or some such shit — and he likes to look like a man of the world so he came to me, see if I could do something. He knows that you and I bullshit over coffee a bit. I said I'd have a word with you. As it happened, I'd heard you were looking for someone."

I said, "Is there anyone in the fucking university who didn't know what was going on? Except in the English department, of course."

"It was a condition I put on my co-operation." Herb smiled. "Simmonds had to be hired on his merits. The only thing he had going for him was an introduction from me to you to get him in the door. Not a recommendation, remember. And I lined up Wanda to pinch-hit."

"Okay. I was desperate, and he did the job, for a few weeks. I still feel like an asshole."

"You look good from where I'm sitting. So let me take this opportunity to suggest a way for you to say fuck the lot of them. Come work for me, Joe. Associate Registrar. Salary: same as Associate Professor. Not as many perks, true. Only three weeks' holiday not three months, but you get the couple of extra weeks at Christmas when the university closes down, all the long weekends, plus two or three little conferences of registrars where you would represent me — there's one in Hawaii this year. How about it?"

"Why?"

"I've had it in mind since you pulled that neat stunt with the diplomas and the Education Minister. This is not your usual academic, I thought. Got his wits about him, this one. I got the okay for an assistant from Bluebell a while ago, but I didn't want to advertise the job until I'd found the right person, someone I'd be sure would stay on my side and look out for me. Then you came along. Bluebell is pleased with you, too, and I don't have a hiring committee to convince."

"When would I start?"

"You free after Christmas?"

"Legally my contract ends in December, though I'm teaching one full-year course, so it's understood that I'll stay around until May."

"Understood by who? Sorry, 'whom.' They could get rid of you at Christmas, right? So fair's fair, you could tell the chairman to stick the job up his jacksie at the end of this term."

"It would be unfair to the students."

"And so say all of us. All right, then. Be magnanimous. That the word? Finish teaching this one course. We'll work your new job around it."

"When will you advertise?"

"Tomorrow."

"When will I be interviewed?"

"That's what we're doing now. Legally, you'll get an offer in about six weeks, after I reply to all the people who will apply in response to the ad. Then you reply accepting it. That what you mean? You'll have your feet under the table by Christmas."

"But I will be able to go home tonight and tell my future wife I've got a job?"

"Don't create any tangles that might get me into trouble. Tell your woman, but don't neither of you say a word to anyone else until you get my offer."

"And the salary scale again?"

"I told you, you rank as an associate professor. I rank as a dean which you can aspire to. I won't last forever."

"Then I'll take it."

"Good. We'll have some fun. Now, tell me if this letter's all right. It's the college's reply to an editorial in the *Globe*, criticising our admission requirements, which the paper seems to think we change depending on the number of applicants. True, of course, we all do it, including our neighbour across town, but see if you can make that a plus."

CAROLE SAID, "NOW LET'S TALK about a new apartment."

I AM BY NATURE AND training a teacher of literature, but they won't let me do that anymore, so I've been offered a nice alternative. I'm not entirely out in the cold. Even Bluebell pays lip service to teaching as our "most important activity." He gives a lecture himself every year to a first year engineering class on the mechanics of sailing, to show how it's done — teaching, not sailing — and he's said that he thinks everyone in administration should have some student contact. So I'm going to twist Jack Cheval's arm, and Herb's, too, to let me teach a course, at night possibly, non-credit probably, perhaps on the uses of the comma.

A NOTE AT THE END

PROFESSOR PETROV'S CAR WAS FOUND a week later by a real estate agent on Summerhill Avenue, in the driveway of a house that was up for sale. The key was in the ignition. There was no fresh damage: the gas tank was full (Vladimir remembered filling it the day before the car disappeared); his tennis racquet and a new can of balls were still on the back seat, and there were two loonies in the ashtray where he kept change for parking meters. That ended the story but did not solve the mystery.

"Kids," the police officer said.

"They didn't go far, did they?"

"Probably just joyriding. Maybe one of them fraternity things. You know, initiation stuff."

Tommy Stokoe said, "I reckon he left it there himself went shopping around there and forgot it probably to the liquor store the guy's a flake —"

"The liquor store has its own parking lot."

"Yeah well maybe he went to Keith's to get his hair cut or to one of those ritzy food shops just south of the liquor store there's no parking there then he had a cup of coffee and caught the subway home see he had some shopping to do and the haircut thing and the liquor store tow you away after an hour don't they so he saw his chance not to have to pay for parking on the street he probably hates parking meters then he came back and couldn't find it in the liquor store lot my guys think that's what happened he just couldn't find it one of my guys says Petrov is a nice guy but he couldn't find his own ass with both hands —"

"What about the keys?"

"Guy like Petrov is always forgetting probably has one taped to the visor one under the floor mat he wouldn't be worried about theft crapbox like that just forgetting his key ring."

"So he kept a key in the car to drive it with?"

"I told you he's a flake maybe he didn't like carrying a lot of keys around."

CAROLE SAID, "THE POLICE ARE right. He left the car unlocked and the key in the ignition, and some kid, maybe, looking to steal something, found the car unlocked, and drove off. Then, when he got to Yonge Street, he saw a cruiser and panicked, turned into Summerhill, and dumped it in the nearest driveway, which just happened to be of a house that was up for sale, and ran. He didn't even take the tennis racquet."

"Not just Vladimir being absent-minded, you don't think?"

"No. Vladimir is embarrassed because now they've found it, he distinctly remembers leaving the car unlocked and the key in the ignition, but he isn't about to say so."